# NOT SO SWEET MARIA
Book 1, Sisters by Marriage

Jessica Spencer

© 2017 to 2023 Gita V. Reddy

ISBN 9781546470694

Disclaimer

This is a work of fiction. Names, characters, businesses, places, events, locales, and incidents are either the products of the author's imagination or used in a fictitious manner. Any resemblance to actual persons, living or dead, or actual events is purely coincidental.

# Table of Contents

# Prologue

*August 1799.*

Mary tiptoed to the door and stood listening outside it. Her dark hair was in curlers and her feet bare under the cotton nightdress. The doctor had come and he was speaking to her nurse.

"Your master died an hour ago. He survived his wife by only six hours."

"What will happen to Mary, Doctor? The missus has a brother but he is in Europe. Who will care for the child?" Gwen asked.

"She has family in England. John made me promise I will send her to his mother. She is a duchess."

"Duchess? Like a queen? The missus never said anything about her."

"I thought John was delirious when he told me his father was the Duke of Severn. But he was coherent. He made me promise, and I shall do everything within my power to send the child to England. Can you accompany Mary? I'll take care of the papers and also provide the money. There will be a manservant going with you."

Mary went back to her room. When Gwen came in, she found her in bed, huddled under the covers, her face to the wall.

The next morning, Gwen was surprised she didn't inquire about her parents like she usually did. She was also relieved; she wouldn't have known how to answer her. Mary was only six but the month spent in quarantine, with only Gwen for company had made her precocious.

Three days later they were on the ship. Mary refused to leave the cabin and clung to Gwen. Gwen told her they were going to live with her grandmother. She didn't know much about the English nobility so she made up stories. She told Mary about the wonderful life she would have with her grandmother. Mary listened but didn't ask questions.

Eight weeks later they were standing outside a mansion that did justice to Gwen's tales.

"I've brought Mr. John's daughter from America," Gwen informed the servant and handed him the doctor's letter. Within no time, they were shown into an enormous room. The duchess came in after an hour.

"Madam, this is Mr. John's daughter, Mary," Gwen said, leading her by the hand.

A footman hissed in her ear. "Not madam! You must say your Grace!"

Gwen barely heard him. She was staring at the richly clad woman who had halted her progress with an imperious hand. She had glanced at Mary and looked away.

"M...my mistress named Mary after her m... mother," Gwen stammered. "It is all in the letter. The Yellow Fever took both my master and mistress."

The duchess cut her short. "She is no longer Mary but Lady Maria. A servant will see you. You may leave the child in her care."

And without sparing her granddaughter another look, the duchess swept out of the room.

# Chapter 1

*London, 1814*

Gareth, Earl of Daventon was in London on business. Not having a taste for Society events, he went to his club. He expected to spend a quiet evening as the *ton* would be busy with balls, soirees, rout-parties and such.

Two tables away, Lord Hennicker sat with his friends. "How does she do it?" he raised his voice and repeated the question.

Lord Hennicker was pleasantly in his cups. His neckcloth had lost its fashionable folds and his eyes, their focus. His friends were also in a similarly pleasurable state.

"How does she do it?" Lord Hennicker slurred for at least the twentieth time, and stood up. He squinted at Daventon and tottered to the earl's table. "Daventon! Nice to see you! Tell me ... how does she do it?"

He lurched backward and Daventon kicked a chair to accommodate him. He would have landed on it but he suddenly slumped forward and hit the table before dropping down on the floor.

His friends came to assist him but were in no condition to be of any real help. Daventon lifted him up and two lackeys miraculously appeared at his side. They knew what to do; it was not uncommon for gentlemen to lose their heads and their feet.

One of Lord Hennicker's companions tried to explain. "Sweet Maria wouldn't have him. Told him she wouldn't have him. Didn't listen. Makes him number four this sennight. And y'know, no one knows …knows…

"How she does it?" the earl added helpfully.

"Has us swarming like bees to honey. How does she do it?"

Gareth did not know and did not want to know. He guessed Sweet Maria was the latest Bird of Paradise. She was probably an actress in Drury Lane and had refused Hennicker's offer of protection.

He had other matters to think about, like the visit to his man of business on the morrow.

***

Sweet Maria was a lady of birth. And Lord Hennicker was not alone in wondering how Lady Maria, or Sweet Maria as the *ton* had christened her, managed to keep all her beaus, even the ones whose suits she had declined, in a fluttering court around her.

She was beautiful but she wasn't the Incomparable of 1814. That title had gone to Lady Phoebe, the youngest daughter of Earl Horlock. She was well dowered but her portion was considerably less than that of Lady Victoria whose grandfather was among the richest men in England and whose father had added to the enormous wealth during his five years in India. Her bloodlines were not impeccable either. Her father, the late Marquess of Roth and owner of sundry other titles had caused a Scandal by marrying an American Commoner.

Four years ago, when Lady Maria made her comeout, no one expected dukes and earls high in the instep to offer for her. After all, she was a Child of Scandal. But she became the most sought-after debutante of the Season. She received three very eligible offers in the first month itself, one of them from a duke in his own right.

It was of no consequence that the Duke of Marcham was old enough to be her grandfather. He was sixty to her eighteen and had indeed been her grandfather's friend. He had lost his heir and the spare in an accident. The young Lady Maria was his choice to rectify that alarming state of affairs.

When she turned down his suit, many match-making mamas rushed in with their charges, some of them vulgarly bragging about the fecundity that ran in their families. To their chagrin, the duke continued with his efforts to make Lady Maria his duchess. So it was with her other suitors. They were not rebuffed by her refusal. Instead, they grew more determined.

Lady Maria was in her fourth Season now and continued to be besieged by offers. At society events, she drew a court around her without any effort. Even the strictest matron couldn't fault her behavior. She neither flirted nor tried to attract attention.

She was somewhat of a trial to the other debutantes. But they could not dislike her. She introduced them to the men around her, and also included them in picnics and promenades. Many of her efforts resulted in the young ladies snagging a husband.

\*\*\*

Gareth crossed over to the window and looked out into the street. His brooding expression did nothing to mar his classical good looks but it made Nat Stevenson nervous. Nat was the recently apprenticed articled clerk of Meyers, Meyers & Meyers. Except for a baron, no peer of the realm had visited the offices since he had joined six months ago.

The baron had barged in and expressed his displeasure in the strongest terms when he had to spend five minutes in the waiting room. His tirade had not ruffled Nate. He was sensible to the baron's consequence. It was the way of the rich and titled to ride roughshod over ordinary folks.

The earl's cool courtesy was a different matter. He had insisted that his business could wait until the surviving member of Meyers, Meyers & Meyers had disposed of the audibly hysterical female closeted in the office. He had also refused the offer of the small private office. Instead, he had sauntered across to the window and was even now negligently leaning against it.

Nat was relieved that my lord did not wish to converse. He grew bold enough to observe him. In spite of his agitation, he had noticed the deep blue eyes and the dark hair, and the sculpted features. Now he took in the six feet two inches frame, the broad shoulders, and the slim hips, shown to advantage in a well-cut olive-green coat, fawn pantaloons, and polished hessians.

He sighed. He would have become a gentleman's gentleman if not for his unfeeling parent who considered his passion for clothes a lot of moonshine. His love for clothes often took him to Half Moon Street and outside opera houses, to ogle at Sprigs of Fashion dressed in the latest mode. The striped waistcoats, the latest style of yellow pantaloons, the boots with jeweled buckles, and the intricately tied neckcloths winking with jewels transported him into a world of ecstasy.

While Nat could not fault my lord's clothing, he wished he had worn a waistcoat of flowered silk and a brighter coat, and favored the fobs and seals that were in fashion. Even the greatcoat he had shrugged off had only a modest number of capes.

Gareth was not aware of the disappointment he had caused young Nat by not aspiring to dandyism. The delicate nature of business that had brought him to his family solicitors occupied his thoughts.

The scandal that had erupted eighteen years ago when he was seven had long ceased to be a topic of discussion among the *haute ton*. But he could not be nonchalant about it; it cut too close to his heart.

A dark carriage stopped across the street. A woman jumped out with lithe grace and a tantalizing display of frills, ankles, and dainty slippers. An older woman followed and lifted a big bag out of the carriage.

When the younger woman made to help her, she slapped away her hand. "No, you don't, my lady!"

Daventon leaned forward, sure he had misheard. The coachman removed two more bags. The young woman said something and laughed. The coachman scowled and the older woman seemed to reprimand the young woman.

The young woman spread her arms wide and lifted her face to the sun and, in the center of the empty street, spun around.

Gareth had enough self-possession not to allow his jaw to drop. The said self-possession came under severe strain when the young woman stopped in mid-twirl and stared at him.

Gareth stared back at the bewitching face with its cream and peaches complexion, large violet eyes and sooty eyelashes, and mouth rounded in surprise.

The woman arched an eyebrow and broke the spell. Daventon blushed. Blushed! As she turned away, she gave him a little smile and swept down her eyelashes.

Minx! Daventon murmured, watching her beguiling progress to a door on the sidewalk. She did not look back again.

He did not know what to think. Her companion had addressed her as a female of rank but a lady wouldn't give strangers arch looks. She wasn't dressed fashionably. Neither was it a fashionable quarter of the city.

He stood at the window, hoping to catch another glimpse of her face. But she stood with her back to him and kept up a conversation with her companion.

The coachman pulled out a key and unlocked a door beside the sidewalk. The young lady continued to converse airily with the other woman and slowly followed her into the room. Gareth felt a stab of disappointment at her obvious indifference to him.

He couldn't be more in the wrong.

***

Maria very much wanted to turn her head. She was sure the devastatingly handsome man was still at the window. She almost felt his gaze on her!

But she knew how disastrous it would be if either Gwen or Adam caught her exchanging looks with the stranger. Gwen would give her a talking to and Adam would refuse to drive her to anyplace he considered unsuitable for a gently bred female of her station.

If the man judged her by her appearance and tried to strike up an acquaintance, Adam would not hesitate to hit him! He was that faithful. He might even inform her grandmother. And the duchess would promptly blame her Commoner mother for her improper behavior.

Maria had only meant to test her theory about bonnets. The straw bonnet was her latest creation. She had worn the bonnet and practiced that arch of the eyebrow in front of the mirror. But the shared moment had turned into something she had never experienced before.

Who was he? Those windows were of a law office but he did not look like a lawyer. In fact, he could not be a lawyer because he was looking out into the street, Lady Maria concluded, impressed by her logical thinking.

Considering his appearance, she listed all the things he could not possibly be. It was amazing. She did have wonderful powers of observation. She had seen him for a moment at a window across the street but was able to recall so much about his person and dress.

By the time Lady Maria came to the end of her frantic mental exercise while maintaining a steady flow of conversation with Gwen, she concluded mournfully he could only be a nobleman. It was too bad! The only interesting man she noticed looked like he belonged to the world she despised.

But scions of noble houses did not visit lawyers' offices in person or stare out into vacant streets. They did not leave their beds at an early hour either unless it was to ride into Hyde Park or watch a madcap curricle race. Therefore, he could not belong to the *haute ton*.

In her fourth Season, she knew everyone who was received by Polite Society. She hadn't met him at any of the balls or soirees. He must be the by-blow of a nobleman.

Pleased with the conclusion that the very personable young man who had discomfited her must be someone unacceptable to the *ton*, Lady Maria turned her thoughts to bonnets.

When she had worn the bonnet and tested the arch look in front of the mirror, it was in the nature of an experiment. Just like two chemicals combined in certain proportions resulted in an explosion, so it was with the bonnet and the flirtatious look.

Trimmed with green lace, decorated with poppies and ferns, the straw bonnet had a sweeping rim and wide red ribbons. The posy was of an unusual design and the bleached straw had an intricate lacy pattern. But what made the bonnet so fetching was the angle at which she had placed the posy and the ribbons clustered into a knot below her left ear.

When she arched her brow, the upward sweep of the bonnet made it more pronounced. A different bonnet would not have enhanced that small gesture. Really, if women understood the language of bonnets, they would have all the men they wanted. Or like in her case, turn down suitors without hurting their sentiments. She always knew which bonnet to wear when a suitor called with a marriage proposal.

She would make a fortune if she took women into her confidence and made them understand that they needed fewer gowns and more bonnets. They needed a bonnet for every occasion. She couldn't do that, however. The magic, the mystique would be lost. And if men learned it was bonnet strings that led them into the parson's trap, the consequences would be disastrous.

While she designed bonnets for women keeping in mind the shape of their face and the coloring, and gave them a list of colors they must wear with the bonnet, she used her secret knowledge only for herself.

The opportunity to send forth the flirtatious look had been unexpected but why had she grown confused? Drat that man! Who was he?

# Chapter 2

As soon as Mr. Meyers was disengaged and learned about the personage in his outer office, he ushered him in personally.

Mr. Meyers was a man of advanced years. Being the family solicitor, he was privy to the family affairs and the Scandal more than most people. However, he did not know the unfortunate circumstances that had led to it.

After exchanging conventionalities, Gareth extracted a slip of paper. "I discovered a codicil to my father's will. He wanted my mother's allowance to be quadruplicated."

Mr. Meyers perused the brief document. It was dated on the very day the late earl had made the lake his watery grave.

"It is not witnessed, my lord," he pointed out.

"That makes no difference. I'm not contesting it."

Mr. Meyers was aware he was not. He had only tried to get out of a daunting task. He knew, as did Gareth, that Lady Daventon would refuse the money. It was a tricky moment. Neither Mr. Meyers nor the earl wanted to indicate in any manner that relations between the countess and her son were strained.

Gareth prepared to leave. "I would appreciate it if my father's last wish was carried out. Please arrange it without upsetting her ladyship."

Four generations of Meyers had taken zealous care of the Daventon fortunes. Naturally, Mr. Meyers felt a connection with the family. He also took a parental interest in Gareth. He had seen him since he was in short coats. It was that sentiment or he was getting senile, he told his wife later, that made him speak up on a private matter.

"My lord, I shall contrive to fulfill the late earl's wishes. However, it is all the same to her ladyship. She barely draws on her allowance. Most of the house is shut up and the grounds are neglected. The estimable woman who was her nurse…"

"Flanders," supplied Gareth.

"She died two months after the earl passed on. Her ladyship has taken it badly. She was never in good spirits after…she was not in the best of health for the past many years but Flanders managed to keep her tolerably well. I visited Wrenrose last week. It was some trifling business but I did not trust Nat with it, seeing that her ladyship leads a retired life."

Mr. Meyers paused and polished his pince-nez. Gareth's fingers on the armrest tightened and his knuckles turned white. However, he masked his agitation under a polite expression.

"I could not meet her ladyship. The housekeeper informed me that she is poorly and refuses to take nourishment. She seems to have lost the will to live. The physician calls every day. He has installed two nurses. They manage to make her take the cordial and the other medicines with great difficulty. The housekeeper, who is a good and loyal servant, wanted to send for you but her ladyship forbade her."

Mr. Meyers tugged at his collar as if it had suddenly grown tight but doggedly came to the end of his piece. "My lord, you should go to her. She has suffered and so had the late earl. Whatever may have transpired, she needs her family around her."

Gareth gave a curt nod and stood up. Mr. Meyers was not deceived. He came around the table and said gently, "Her ladyship's condition is not desperate. I called upon the physician. She does not suffer from any ailment. All she needs is a change of scene. Wrenrose is far too gloomy."

Gareth briskly walked out of the office and climbed into the hack he had kept waiting. At the same moment the women he had seen earlier emerged out of the door. He was gratified to observe that the young woman was looking up at the window. He leaned back with a perplexed frown. How had he been mistaken? She did not appear a whit saucy. She looked demure and innocent. Who was she?

He rarely came to London during the Season but it was not likely a debutante would visit the business section, and that too early in the day. Morning hours were meant for promenades in Hyde Park in fashionable walking dresses and shopping expeditions in Bond Street.

But, in spite of her ordinary gown, she looked like Quality. The way she carried herself, the tilt of her head, her self-possession, and the deference of her companions seemed like she had blue blood in her veins. It was possible her family had suffered a change of fortune.

But a gentlewoman would not work in a shop. He didn't like to think it but the only other explanation left was she was the natural daughter of some nobleman. It was not uncommon for members of the nobility to sire children outside wedlock. Sometimes the children were provided for and given an education. That could account for the woman's bearing and her having to earn a living.

He wondered what the establishment was. When the hack turned on to the main road, he craned his neck out the window to read the signboard. The shop had neither a signboard nor a display window. But there were two carriages outside it, one of which bearing the Somerset crest. As the Somersets were models of propriety, Gareth concluded that the establishment was a respectable one.

His thoughts did not linger over the mystery woman for long. Mr. Meyers had painted an alarming picture of his mother's health. On his father's demise, he had sent a messenger to his mother, to inform her of the funeral, which was to be a small affair given the nature of the demise. She hadn't come nor had she sent a reply.

A week later, Flanders had written that the countess was distraught and not in a condition to travel or receive her son. She had promised to write again.

That letter had wounded him. After his father's death, he had hoped to reconcile with his mother. He hadn't forgotten her parting words. Eighteen years ago, before leaving, she had held him close and said, "I'll always love you! Remember that. Take care of your sister and respect your father. He is a good man. Good but mistaken!"

When Flanders did not write again, he had used anger to hide his hurt. He had decided that his mother did not care for them any longer. He had sulked like a schoolboy and blamed her for everything, including his father's death. When he had discovered the codicil to his father's will, he had thought to use it as a pretext to visit her. But it had seemed safer to see Mr. Meyers instead.

He regretted not going to Wrenrose. Had death not snatched her away, Flanders would have kept her word and written to him. He remembered her from his boyhood. She was equally his nurse as his mother's. He had missed her sharp tongue and kind heart as much as he had been lost without his mother's gentle presence.

He would go to Wrenrose but first, he would write to the physician for his opinion. Having decided upon his course of action, he went to White's and sent the letter.

***

While coming out of the club, Gareth walked smack into Lord Barrington. "Gareth! No, you are Daventon now. Sorry about your father. I wanted to come to the funeral but could not."

"Always Gareth to you, my boy! How could you come when your nuptials were a week away? I regret I could not be your groomsman. Marriage suits you. You look civilized. Lady Barrington is to be congratulated on accomplishing so difficult a feat."

"You shall congratulate Amy in person. Have you lunched?"

"I have. I will do myself the honor of calling upon her ladyship tomorrow morning."

"You shall do no such thing! You are my oldest friend and Amy will have my head if I don't present you immediately. You will be doing me a favor. She is sorely in need of some diversion."

Lord Daventon's eyebrows shot up. "Amy's bored to tears. The physician has forbidden her from stepping out of the house. She's in a delicate condition," Lord Barrington explained.

"My felicitations!"

"She has grown irritable and frets the daylights out of me."

"I remember you writing to me a year ago that she was the most amiable of creatures."

"You know I met Amy at a village assembly and married her after a short engagement. We left for Scotland after the wedding. Three months ago, Amy decided we would come to London because she hadn't had a Season. Not wanting her to feel cheated of all the balls and soirees, I agreed. She spent a month preparing. You won't believe the amount of clothes and gee-gaws she ordered. Beggared me, in fact," Lord Barrington grumbled about the expense but his tone was indulgent.

Gareth didn't miss the light of love in his friend's eyes. Barrington was besotted with his wife. He hoped Amy returned his sentiments. Unreciprocated love was a corrosive acid. Who knew it better than him?

"Amy said none of the gowns from her trousseau were of the first stare and she would look a positive fright if she ventured out in any of them. I didn't know it took so many people to rig out a lady for a Season. I accompanied her to dressmakers, mantua makers, milliners, haberdashers, and wherever she wanted to go. No sooner did her new gowns arrive, she started feeling sick. She did not get to wear above half a dozen of those gowns. That has made her miserable. This morning I told her she could wear them at home and she bit my head off. I escaped for a breath of fresh air. As luck would have it, I ran into you."

Gareth leaned back in the curricle and let Lord Barrington run on in a similar vein. He had always been an incessant talker. At Eton, while some of the other boys told him to shut up, Gareth took refuge in his prattle. It saved him from questions about the Scandal.

***

Lady Barrington was indeed in the dumps and though she said she was charmed that her husband had brought home a friend, she did not look it. "James, I will go mad if I don't do anything interesting."

"Shall I check for the latest Minerva Press novel in the library?"

"I don't want to read or sew. I want something to cheer me up. I want a new bonnet!"

"That shouldn't be difficult. Send your maid for one of those caps, though why you wear them is beyond me. They make you look a fright, luv."

His lady answered him with a screech and flung a cushion at his head. Then she burst into tears.

Lord Daventon felt himself decidedly *de trop*. He wished he could walk out of the room without taking leave of her ladyship only that would make him appear a boor.

Lord Barrington rushed to his lady's side and tried to calm her. He got down on his knees. Gareth winced. Those pantaloons must be making him deuced uncomfortable!

"Now, now, I didn't mean you look a fright luv! These caps will make anyone look queer!"

His lady tugged at the strings of the frilly confection on her head but only succeeded in getting them into a snarl. "This morning you said I looked divine! The chintz curtains set my gown and c.cap to great advantage!"

After a few more accusations, my lady's sobs turned into hiccups, then sniffles. She wiped her nose on a wisp of lace, and when her husband offered his snowy-white handkerchief, inelegantly blew her nose, and told him in no uncertain words to stay away from her forever because she looked a fright. For good measure, she thrust the handkerchief back into his hand. Barrington retreated to the end of the room, for all the world looking like a whipped hound.

The scene was fast turning into one out of a Cheltenham tragedy. Gareth could have slipped out without the principal actors noticing his exit but he had to help his friend; more so because he knew how to. Years of coaxing his sister Laura out of the dismals had taught him the right words. He walked up to Lady Barrington and offered her his handkerchief. She stared at it mutinously. She really was like Laura, he thought, with a surge of affection.

"My friend is a boor. You don't have to ruin your beautiful complexion on his account."

She sniffed but took the proffered handkerchief and dabbed at her tears. Her husband took a tentative step in her direction. "You are heartless and I hate you!" she told him.

Before Barrington could again put his foot in his mouth, Gareth said, "Don't forgive him. I can see from his face he wants to apologize."

Barrington caught the hint and rushed forward. He folded his tall lanky frame into a spindle-legged chair beside the chaise and said, clumsily, "My dear, I should not have said that. You don't look a fright at all. What I meant was they don't flatter you …

Daventon cleared his throat and James caught his frown. "…as much as they should. I like to see your hair, it's nice and I like it. I think it looks like…"

"Silk", mouthed Daventon.

"Milk."

"What? How can my hair look like milk? Are you foxed, sir?"

"Silk!" mouthed the earl again.

"Silk! Your hair is like silk!" Barrington exclaimed, taking Lady Barrington's hands in his own.

"Oh James! That is exactly what you said when you courted me! You are right! These lace caps make me look hideous! Will you please get me a new bonnet?"

"Me?"

"Lady Edwina called this morning. She wore a most enchanting creation and also brought me such exciting news! She knows who makes Lady Maria's bonnets!" Lady Barrington clasped her hands and looked at her husband. A peevish look replaced the triumphant one.

"Don't tell me you don't know what I'm talking about! Remember I told you I must have a bonnet like the one Lady Maria wore to the Circulating Library?"

"You told me you wish you had not purchased so many bonnets."

"Silly man! That was later when I was not able to wear them! I told you about Lady Maria's ravishing bonnets the week we arrived. They are a rage with all the ladies. Miss Evenstone, a most resourceful young lady, made a sketch of Lady Maria's bonnet for Mme. Chevalier to copy."

"Mme. Chevalier?"

"The milliner on Bond Street! That's where I got my bonnets trimmed. Mme. Chevalier made a bonnet from the sketch but it wasn't the same at all. Then someone asked Lady Maria directly. She was obliging enough to give the address. Now everyone is ordering bonnets from her. Lady Edwina has three. She wore one this morning and it became her very well. She is such a dull creature but the bonnet gave her face so much animation. She has never looked better! She said it was a pity that bonnets aren't allowed will ball gowns. James, I must have a bonnet trimmed by this woman. I have hankered after one for so long."

"Sure, luv. I don't see the problem. Do you think I would grudge you a bonnet? What made you think I'd turned into such a nipfarthing fellow? Send your maid for one."

"Lady Edwina says the dratted woman has a long waiting list. She is refusing fresh orders. I want you to use your title and get me a bonnet otherwise I'm going myself."

"Amy, the younger son of a duke is of no use if you need him to throw a title around. Should I ask my father? He's in town and he indulges you. He could visit this woman and threaten to have her in front of the House of Lords for not selling you a bonnet."

The sally was met with another cushion flung at his head. He beat a hasty retreat. Lord Daventon stayed back to elicit the address of the milliner. He assured Lady Barrington that her husband would, if need be, wrest a bonnet from the milliner, and bade her obey the physician's orders like a good child.

Lady Barrington answered him with a fresh bout of tears and assured him that she was not such a watering pot or a shrew. It was just that he put her in mind of her dear brother, Thomas, and James was being such a brute and would he please call her Amy because Lady Barrington sounded horrid.

# Chapter 3

"Daventon, how does a shop do business if it does not have a sign?" Lord Barrington demanded unreasonably of his friend, staring at the hastily scrawled note in his wife's hand. It directed them to a dull part of London in which they were to seek out the 'Corner Shop without a Sign on the Door.'

"I may know of this establishment. I visited my lawyer's offices this morning and saw the Somerset carriage outside a corner shop in the street. It did not display a sign."

Fortunately, Lord Barrington did not have an active curiosity. He did not ask what made his friend notice such an insignificant detail. Moreover, locating the shop was not the real problem. He balked at shopping for fripperies in a poky shop that was the rage and would undoubtedly have a gaggle of women fighting over satin roses and plumes.

But his lady could not be denied. Since she was increasing, a change had come over her. The sweet young woman who never tired of pleasing him had become a shrew. No, not a shrew, he told himself loyally but could not think of a less offending epithet either.

"Daventon, you must come with me."

"Must I?"

"Dash it, I can't go in there alone. The curst woman would wonder why I was buying bonnets. She would think it was for a Cyprian. It would not be the thing at all. In fact, it would be an insult to Amy and if it reached her ears, she would make herself ill with worry."

"You could tell Amy the truth!"

"How could I when she will not ask me to the face! I'm not such an addlepate that I will deny a rumor. That will be the surest way of making her think it is true. Women are like that. Tell them something is not true and they will believe you are hiding the truth from them."

"Then tell her it is the truth."

"She will believe it and it will break her heart which she does not deserve. Neither do I because I have no mistress!"

"And if I accompany you?"

"Why, everyone with think it's for your High Flyer."

"You don't much care about that."

"It will add to your consequence. You are sadly wanting in that direction. Always thought so."

Lord Daventon's lips twitched at his friend's farfetched tale. He did not think the less of him for being hen-hearted about plunging into so feminine a domain. He would go with him but not in broad daylight. That would be too conspicuous.

"James, if you can postpone your visit for later, I'll accompany you. I have to call upon my aunt's friend now. Shall we go into the shop at er...closing time?"

Lord Barrington was by no means a slow top. He saw the wisdom of his friend's suggestion; gently bred females did not visit shops at late hours.

He warmly shook his friend's hand and insisted that Lord Daventon take his curricle as he didn't need it. He had nowhere to go and could not return home without the bonnet. He would read the newspapers at the club. Or tear his hair out in the peace of an all-men's bastion.

*** 

On the eve of Lord Daventon's departure to London, his aunt Lady Helena had given him a commission. "Gareth, I have received a letter from my dear friend Harriet. She is the Duchess of Severn and is in London for the Season."

"When did you receive the letter, Aunt Nell? I didn't see it in the post."

Turning a guilty pink, Lady Helena blustered her way out of the tight corner. "That is of no import! You are going to London tomorrow. It is a happy coincidence that Lady Severn has opened her townhouse for the Season. You must call on her."

"Does she have a daughter, Aunt Nell?"

"A granddaughter. From what I hear, you will suit," Lady Helena answered eagerly, forgetting to dissemble.

"Since when did you turn matchmaker, dearest?"

"Gareth, it is time you wed. I was hoping you would fix your interest on the baron's daughter. But Lydia is betrothed to her brother's friend."

26

"Must I wed because Lydia is getting married?"

"You must marry for your sister's sake. Your wife can launch her into Polite Society. I have lived a retired life all these many years. I can chaperon her but Laura needs someone closer to her age. She is rather shy and doesn't make friends easily."

Laura was eighteen. While Gareth had gone to Eton and Oxford, she'd never left home. Apart from Lydia, she didn't have any friends. She had no memories of her mother but the gossip had wounded her and made her fearful of Society.

"You know I'll do anything for Laura."

"I hope you will fall in love with a good woman and make her your countess."

"Daventons are unlucky in love," he had answered.

"Enough of that fustian! Your father spoke a lot of nonsense when he was in his cups!"

"You sat up with him when he got maudlin. Are all Daventons devoted to their siblings, I wonder?"

"They are!" Lady Helena said, turning the jest to her advantage. "That's why you must wed soon. Lady Harriet and I have maintained a steady correspondence. In her last letter, she suggested a match between you and her granddaughter, provided you are both agreeable. I replied that you will call and pay your addresses to her granddaughter when you visit London."

Gareth had decided he would consent to the match if the duchess' granddaughter turned out to be a sensible young woman. He did not want a romantic chit who would look for love; love was the plague and he was determined to avoid it like one.

Lord Daventon was an enigma to most people. Not given to excesses of any kind, he did not follow the usual pursuits of the *beau monde*. He was handsome, intelligent, wealthy, and heir to an earldom. He attended enough society events not to be labeled a recluse, and was punctilious in his address. While he did not discomfit hostesses by retiring into the cardroom or standing out a great number of dances, no young lady could claim to have won his marked favor. Neither could the young widows looking for discreet liaisons or the bored married women in need of well-earned compensation for putting up with boorish or aged husbands claim to have netted the handsome lord.

***

Gareth presented himself at the imposing Severn House. In spite of it not being the fashionable hour for receiving visitors, he was ushered into the presence of the duchess within minutes of presenting his card.

The Duchess of Severn made no pretense of examining him. Though she did not raise a quizzing glass, he was sure she did not miss much. She appraised him for a whole minute and offered her claw-like-hand for him to kiss. He could not imagine her as his aunt's contemporary; she looked very old.

She answered his unasked question. "Lady Helena is my dear friend's daughter. That's right. Your grandmother was my friend. You don't look like her at all."

Gareth inclined his head and took the chair indicated by the duchess. "You look like your father," she continued. "He was a handsome devil. I never saw him after he sold Daventon House. It was the last house in this lane. He sold it to a Cit. He wasn't thinking straight at that time but it was a terrible thing to do to all of us. We had a coal merchant going past our houses in flashy carriages. His wife once hailed me. Naturally, I looked through her. A pity she didn't understand I was cutting her."

Over tea, the duchess asked questions that could have been impertinent coming from anyone else. He suspected she was trying to intimidate him. While accepting a buttered scone, he politely inquired whether she would present him to her granddaughter. "My aunt is particularly keen that I make her acquaintance."

The duchess did not miss his meaning. She sagely nodded her turbaned head and said she was glad Lady Helena had spoken to him because there was no need to beat about the bush. "Matches are best decided between families. Young people often make a mess of them by dragging in sentimental nonsense. The gel is out to buy a bonnet from a new shop. They are the rage, I believe. You may speak to her tomorrow."

Gareth took leave and drove back to the club. If the girl was as hard-faced as her grandmother, he would marry her. Though he quailed at the thought of sitting across a grim-faced antidote for the rest of his life, she would suit his purpose. Perhaps she would not be an antidote. The duchess must have been attractive in an imposing sort of way.

It was better if she was an antidote, he chastised himself. He would marry and do his duty, that was all. A wife well-connected would help Laura in finding an eligible husband and that was all he wanted. There was no need for him and his wife to live in each other's pockets.

He would not be his father. A practical arrangement was better than marrying someone he loved and worrying that his love was not returned.

He loved his sister. He felt responsible for her and a little guilty that he had enjoyed six more years of their mother's love. He had memories of his mother's soft touch. He remembered that she had loved him whereas Laura had no recollections whatsoever.

For years he used to dream that a cloaked and masked man stole into his room in the middle of the night and robbed him of his biggest treasure. The treasure took different forms but even in his dreams, he knew the man had come to snatch his mother.

***

Lord Barrington was waiting impatiently at the club for him. "Shall we go? The shop may keep early hours and where will that leave us?" He did not want to take the curricle. "We will take a hack," he said, "an open curricle is not quite the thing at this hour."

Gareth did not dispute his friend's strange notion of gentility. He hailed a cab and gave the directions. Lord Barrington raised another objection. "We mustn't stop in front of the shop. Better to get down a little away and observe."

Gareth complied with the wishes of his harried friend. They waited on the street across the shop. Its door was mysteriously shut and its windows curtained. A Lady of Quality and her maid stood outside the shop. The lady was tall and though her features were regular and ringlets clustered around her forehead, she was of a stern appearance. Her chin was square and she held her head at a haughty angle. Daventon was sure she was the duchess' granddaughter. She even had the same nose. She was the woman he was sent to court!

He watched her and felt no stirring of attraction. There was no danger of falling in love with her. He had been afraid on that count because Aunt Helena had said, "I've made inquiries. The girl is a diamond of the first water. You must court her and marry her. You are far too serious, my dear. A pretty wife is the cure!"

A carriage stopped across the road and the women left in it.

"They must be the last customers. Shall we go in?" Lord Barrington hissed.

The shop door was closed. Daventon knocked. There was no answer. He gave the door a little push. It was locked from within.

"The shop is shut. We'll have to come tomorrow," he said.

"You know I can't do that! Amy will accuse me of making up a Banbury tale! I must see about the dratted bonnet now. There must be someone inside. I saw a light within when we drove past."

Gareth remembered the side entrance. Leaving his friend at the front door, he went to have a look. Two women were standing on the pavement, opposite the door. Fortunately, the street was lit, and he made out the two women he had seen that morning. If he hurried, there was hope yet for Amy's bonnet.

The older woman saw him coming purposefully towards them and rushed at him. Then, most unexpectedly, she whacked her reticule over his head! He staggered but did not go down. As the virago came at him again, he managed to grasp her wrist. She struggled and cried out. He let go of her wrist only after she'd dropped the reticule.

He picked it up from the pavement. "My good woman, what does it contain? Rocks?"

The woman looked daggers at Gareth and stood in front of the young woman in a protective stance. The young woman stepped from behind her.

The light from the gas lamp fell obliquely on her face, illuminating three-quarters of it. With her chiseled features and lustrous eyes, and curls undone, she looked like a painting he had seen in a small gallery on the Continent. The rest of her came into focus. A pulse fluttered at the base of her throat, and her bosom heaved.

"My lady, don't be alarmed! I mean no harm!" he exclaimed.

The older woman frowned. "You mustn't address my …friend like that. She is not a titled lady."

"I thought I heard you address your companion as 'my lady'," Gareth said before recollecting that he ought not to disclose the morning's encounter.

The young woman smiled brightly. "That's my name, kind sir. I'm Milady. I fear there has been a mistake. Gwen hit you because she thought you were trying to accost us.".

Gwen glowered and took Lady Maria's arm. "Humph! I was only being careful. Look here, we are not alone. Our coachman is just around the corner, getting a wheel oiled. You better be off before he arrives."

"Are you connected with this bonnet shop? I'm here with Lord Barrington. We came on a delicate business. His wife is in a delicate condition and the physician has ordered her to rest. She has instructed her husband, Lord Barrington, to bring her a bonnet. We knew the shop would be filled with women during the day. Shopping for a bonnet among so many women was..."

"Delicate?" Lady Maria supplied, without a quiver in her voice.

"Yes. No. Lord Barrington thought he would have to explain his wife's..."

"Delicate condition?"

"Er, yes."

Lord Barrington got tired of trying the door. "Gareth!" he called, rounding the corner.

Lady Maria lowered the veil of her bonnet over her face. "Please tell Lady Barrington someone from the shop will call on her tomorrow. She must not get into a pet."

The carriage arrived at the precise moment. Without another word, she almost ran into it.

"Who was that?" Lord Barrington asked.

"I don't know. She is either the owner of the shop or an assistant. She promised to send someone to see your wife about the bonnet."

"Wonderful! Why was she running away?"

"I don't know. She must be in a hurry. Let's go."

\*\*\*

"That was a narrow escape!" Gwen scolded. "Lord Barrington knows you well. He would have recognized you!"

"He wouldn't have."

"You mean because of the veil? That was quick thinking but it was a matter of luck you were wearing a bonnet with a veil."

"Gwen, people see what they expect. He would not have expected to see Lady Maria in a simple gown with a working girl's bonnet in this unfashionable part of London."

"You and your disguises! One day someone will recognize you and the duchess will have my head! It's a good thing she doesn't venture out much and there's nobody to tell her you sometimes disappear after a dance or two."

Adam drove them to a small house. The ducal carriage was waiting there. Gwen helped Lady Maria change back into her ball gown and they returned home with no one any wiser.

***

Lady Maria did not sleep for a long time. Her thoughts were all about the handsome gent who had crossed her path twice. After she had seen him in the morning, his direct blue gaze had followed her for a long time.

After engaging in speech with him, she was struck by how different he was from the gentlemen she was accustomed to meeting. She smiled when she recollected his abashed looks as he explained Lord Barrington's predicament.

Men of the *ton* were generally arrogant. Their speech was either pompous or inane. They dressed like peacocks in gaudy waistcoats and even preened like the showy birds. But *he* was elegance personified.

She had her reasons for not wanting to marry anyone from the *ton*. Sometimes, she had wondered what she would do if she was courted by a gentleman that she found interesting and wanted to wed. Fortunately, that had never happened and she had gently turned down all offers.

Lord Barrington had called him Gareth. Gareth was an unusual name but she liked it. It was nice and strong. She wondered if he was Lord Barrington's secretary. That would explain his presence in the lawyer's office.

If his father was a Cit or even a worker in the docks, it would be a point in his favor because that would put the Duchess of Severn's nose severely out of joint. But it was unlikely Lord Barrington would engage someone from a low social order or of questionable birth. Perhaps, he was the son of a vicar.

\*\*\*

Lady Maria had no illusions about her place in Society. Her beauty and manners would have fetched her naught if the duchess did not exercise so much influence.

Maria was fiercely proud of her father. He had spurned the advantages of birth and title for the sake of love. She clung to the memories of her parents. Luckily, she had their likeness. It was her most treasured possession. Gwen had thought to bring it when they left the plantation. Often, she asked Gwen to tell her about her parents. She knew they loved music and books. She would happily sell her soul to hold a book that had belonged to them.

But she had nothing! Nothing at all! The duchess had sold the plantation years ago and hadn't bothered to have anything shipped to England. It proved she did not care for her son – actually, her stepson.

Maria hated the palatial house in which she had grown up. The portrait gallery had likenesses of generations of Severns, all with smug faces and arrogant smiles, except for the last portrait that was her father's. The duke had removed it but after his death, the duchess had restored it. There was no portrait of her mother.

Even after fifteen years, Maria still considered America her true home. She dreamed of returning and buying back the plantation. If she could not regain the plantation, she would settle in France and open her own establishment. To this end, she was already earning from the shop and saving every penny.

She was six months short of being twenty-one and in her fourth Season. If the *ton* did not know about the proposals she received, they would have pitied her, or mocked her for not snagging a husband. She wanted to stay unattached for the duration of the Season. Once she was twenty-one, she would sail away to America. The duchess would not be able to stop her.

Maria had not thought beyond that. A husband had never figured in her plans. But that night she dreamed of one, and he had blue eyes, and his name was Gareth.

# Chapter 4

Severn House was a handsome, well-appointed house with the park noted for its beauty and elegance. Designed by Lancelot "Capability" Brown in the early eighteenth century, it was among the best maintained gardens in London.

Lady Maria's window gave her a panoramic view of the lush lawns, gravel paths, fountains, and artistically placed stone benches. Being an unfashionably early riser, it also allowed her –the fickle weather permitting - to watch the sun rise.

Gwen knew of her penchant of sitting by the open window. She entered through the dressing room and draped a wrap around her charge, softly grumbling about young people who did not know any better than to catch a summer chill.

"What ails you, lambie?" she asked in concern for Maria looked unusually serious.

"Gwen, I have not heard back from that man I wrote to. I don't know how much longer I can avoid getting married. Honestly, what is it with these gentlemen? I don't encourage their suit and yet I receive offers."

"Did anyone propose yesterday? I thought Lord Hennicker was the last."

"I know Lord Hardwick will be next. We were away from home most of yesterday. He called twice and left hideously large bouquets. I'm sure he will be our first caller and will propose. He had that look in his eye when he asked for a dance."

Gwen made sympathetic sounds as she added a gown with a torn flounce to the mending basket.

"Hearing out Lord Hennicker was ordeal enough. He wouldn't leave my hands and he wouldn't get off his knees. I was mortified someone would come into the salon. Thank God it was you!"

"I suspected something was not right when I saw his sister and mother came out of the salon. I'd seen his friends leave before them. I guessed it was a ruse to leave you alone with Lord Hennicker."

"Gwen, the duchess is growing impatient. I see it in her face. If I do not hear from Mr. Stubbs, we will book a passage and go to America."

"My dear, do you not think it would be better to wed and then visit America?"

"My dear, you are getting to be as bad as the duchess. You taught me what it means to be an independent American. How can you wish me to become the wife of an English lord? He will despise my mother and it will be worse than living with her grace because I will not be able to avoid him."

"My dear, surely, if he loves you, he will love every part of your life and take you to visit America. You will have a great deal of money and can buy back your parents' plantation."

"Gwen, you have spent fifteen years in England but you have not understood the *ton*. They do not marry for love. They do not forget a scandal, and they do not forgive anyone who breaks their rules. The duke turned away my father and refused to meet my mother. If he had accepted them, they would not have caught that fever. They would be alive today. It's their fault that I am an orphan."

"They could not know," Gwen said, trying to calm down Maria. "The dresser tells me the duchess tried her best. She cared very much for your father though she was his step-mama."

"That's a lot of fustian and you know it! Gwen, you needn't help me if you don't want to. I am making more money than I thought possible with my bonnets. As soon as I hear from Mr. Stubbs, I shall pay him for the plantation and sail to America. Your precious duchess had no business selling it in the first place. It belonged to me!"

At first, on their arrival from America, Gwen had kept herself aloof from the other servants. She had devoted herself to looking after Maria, the little orphan girl who would not leave her side. She had thought the duchess cold and blamed her and the late duke for driving away their son. Now she did not know who was to blame. Perhaps, no one.

Every Severn heir had chosen his bride with care, giving importance above all to lineage. The Severn brides had all come from ancient families and had done their duty of producing heirs with the family jaw and nose. His Grace, the Duke of Severn, had himself settled upon Lady Amelia as his bride because her blood was almost as blue as his own. She had died in childbed and five years later, he married Lady Harriet, once again from an impeccable family.

For his son, he had sifted through the ancestries of the best families and decided that Lady Theodosia would be the suitable vessel for the next generation of Severns. He did not have the least doubt that his heir would accept his choice. Without waiting for him to return from the Continent, he gave his word to Lady Theodosia's sire, a royal duke, that the families would be connected by ties of marriage.

By then the marquess had already pledged his troth to the refreshingly lovely Janet Thornton who did not simper or resort to artifice. She did not hanker after his title either, in fact, she did not know about it because he was traveling as plain Mr. John Marvel who was down on his luck.

The first thing he did on receiving his father's summons was to marry the woman of his choice. Ten days later he presented his father with the *fait accompli*. The duke was furious at the preposterous idea of mingling common blood with the Severn bloodline. He ordered the marquess to annul the marriage and offered to pay off the 'hussy' and when that failed, he threatened to disinherit his son.

The marquess, in addition to the Severn nose and jaw, had also inherited his share of stubbornness. Instead of trying to conciliate his sire, he chose to turn his back on his heritage.

He left his home and country and sailed to America where he bought a plantation and lived happily as Mr. John Marvel, husband to Janet Marvel, and doting father to Mary Marvel. Unfortunately, he did not live for long.

Gwen was in their employ. She had married young. When she was nineteen, her husband was killed in a saloon brawl. Destitute and close to starvation, she had reached the Marvel's plantation, looking for work. They had taken her in as a servant. Soon she had become Mary's nanny.

A year later, a virulent fever swept through the plantations killing master and servant alike. The servants who were not afflicted ran away. Gwen stayed. On the doctor's orders, she quarantined herself and Mary in a room opening into the back garden. Good food, exercise, sunshine, and an Indian's preventive draught saved them both.

Mary's father had become delirious to the end. He had begged the doctor to send his daughter to England, to his mother who was the Duchess of Severn.

Gwen had expected Mary's grandmother to enfold Mary in love and comfort her for the loss of her parents. Instead, she was cold and dismissive.

Mary was terrified of the woman with grey hair and piercing silver eyes. Gwen had shelved her plans of returning to America. She had stayed on, prickly like a thorn, and suspicious of the duchess.

Mary hated everything about her opulent new home. She begged Gwen to take her back. Gwen did not know what to do. She was not sure it would be the right thing to take the child away from the advantages that were hers. She began telling her they would wait until she was older. She would save her wages and they would return 'home.'

Mary, whom the duchess rechristened Maria after the late duke's mother, became a model child. She was docile and industrious. But it was only a mask. Within, she was fired with a goal. Like her father, she would also renounce wealth and spurn her place in society and return to her mother's land. Gwen had promised to take her.

When she was older, she knew she was rich. Her overflowing jewelry box told her that. A couple of diamond clips were enough to buy passage for Gwen and her. A few more pieces and they could start a new life in America. But Gwen had told her so many stories about the American way of life and the American spirit where people worked and made their own fortune that Maria thought she understood why her father had rejected wealth in favor of his plantation.

Lady Severn took care to see she was brought up as a young lady befitting her station. She appointed governesses and tutors who reported on her progress. Beyond that, she barely took notice of her.

When Mary was still a little girl, she overheard the duchess speak disparagingly of her American mother. The words entered her heart like poison darts. The visitors who descended in droves to pay their respects to her departed father were no better. They stared at her and spoke ill of her mother. On one occasion, two frightening old women examined her face and pronounced it free from bad blood.

Mary grew up to consider the *ton* and the duchess her enemies. From a young age she abhorred their hypocrisy. She blamed the duchess for everything. She considered her a cold woman who had driven away her stepson. Often, she thought if the duchess was her father's own mother, she would not have let him leave.

She did not care that she was a great success in society. When she made her come out, the Duke of

Marcham had referred to her as 'that sweet child, Lady Maria.' The haute monde had quickly coined the epithet Sweet Maria. Her beauty and the animation in her face drew the men, while her correct behavior found favor with the women. She was Sweet Maria, and in fashion even in her fourth Season.

*** 

Maria's love for sewing arose out of necessity. She had brought across three of her dolls from America. The nursery in the ducal house was filled with dolls and toys. She explored them sometimes but played with her 'own' dolls, nursed them, and looked after them. She decided it was unfair she had so many clothes and her dolls had to do with only one set. She set about making clothes for them. Gwen was a skilled needlewoman. She showed her how to make frocks and bonnets for the dolls.

One of her governesses was a remarkable scholar. When she discovered an insatiable thirst for knowledge in her pupil, she taught her unconventional subjects like mathematics.

By her thirteenth year, Mary, or Lady Maria as she was called, was equally passionate about designing bonnets and geometry and learned to fuse the two. She experimented with drawing different shapes of faces and discovered how a clever bonnet could change a person's face and transform the wearer's personality. The angle of a feather, the tilt of the brim, the shape or width of the ribbon, the lace and the net, there were so many ways one could transform an average face into something that drew glances.

Gowns followed the dictates of fashion but bonnets, bonnets created personalities.

During her first Season, Gwen found a skilled seamstress who was down on her luck. Mme. Brigitte belonged to an émigré family. She could not speak much English and was finding it difficult to get work. Gwen, on behalf of her mistress, set her up in a tiny shop, recruited another woman to assist her, and a boy to do the odd jobs and deliveries. Mme. Brigitte made bonnets to Lady Maria's designs and supplied them to another Frenchwoman who had her own shop in Bond Street. Mme. Brigitte thought she was working for Gwen.

Gwen had gone to all this trouble because Lady Maria threatened to open a shop herself if she did not help her.

The coachman, Adam, who had been the late Earl's boyhood friend, was the only one in on the secret. He knew of her plans to sail to America and was determined to thwart them. Like Gwen, he hoped she would wed soon and drop her preposterous scheme about running a plantation or settling in France.

*** 

When in London, the Duchess of Severn was not an early riser. Therefore, her summons to Lady Maria to join her for breakfast in the dining room caused a flutter.

Maria was working on a new design for a bonnet. She was dressed in a simple round gown and surrounded by sheets of paper. The summons had Gwen and her maid bustling around her, fussing over her clothes and hair. Half an hour later, she walked into the dining room, looking demure in a sprigged yellow muslin gown edged with green lace, with a wide sash setting off her trim waist. Short ringlets framed her face while long curls trailed down her left shoulder. Her slippers had green tassels and ribbons matching her dress.

Her Grace came in five minutes later. Maria dropped into an exquisite curtsey that was quite unnecessary, except that it emphasized the distance between them. They completed breakfast in silence, neither doing justice to the dishes on the sideboard.

The duchess dismissed the servants and Lady Maria readied herself for the talk. She knew Lady Severn was growing impatient. This was her fourth season, and though the duchess disliked London, she came every year to lend countenance to the Child of Scandal.

Lady Maria chose a straight-backed chair. Spreading her skirts evenly, she clasped her hands loosely in her lap and raised clear violet eyes to the duchess.

"How beautiful she is! How well she hides herself! If only we could be friends!" the duchess thought. She well knew the docile appearance was a mask. Maria was a different person when she was with Gwen, or with the younger maids. She took after her father that way. John had been on easy terms with the gardener's boy and the coachman's children. It had annoyed his father no end.

John's death had left her bereft. The shock, and Maria's startling resemblance to her mother had prevented her from befriending the child. There was also the fear of hurt; she had loved John with her whole heart and he had spurned her; she did not want to love another child.

But love had crept in. By then it was too late to get past the wall of reserve between them. Maria had grown into a fiercely proud young woman who seemed to hold her in disdain. Her icy politeness conveyed as much.

"Lady Maria, you have turned down a fair number of eligible men. Are your affections fixed elsewhere?"

"Your Grace, I have not formed any attachment."

"Why have you not accepted any of the proposals? Does your birth make you reject your suitors? You may rest on that count. You are a Severn."

Lady Maria seethed at the implied insult to her mother but did not say anything.

"Do you know gentlemen are placing bets in White's about you? There is a wager going about who will propose next and whether you will accept him. Your behavior has caused your name to be bandied about in a most unseemly manner. With your unfortunate circumstances, you cannot be seen to be frivolous."

Lady Maria turned a little pale and her eyes grew bright but the mask of polite deference stayed in place.

"The Earl of Daventon called yesterday," the duchess continued. "He is a most personable young man though there is some scandal in his family. Not about his birth, his bloodlines are unsullied but the late earl cast away his mother. No one knows why. Rumors have it that she behaved with a total lack of propriety but I don't believe it. Lady Daventon was a sweet, well-behaved child, without any guile. She loved her husband and children."

Lady Maria knew of it. It was the biggest Scandal after her father wed a commoner.

"I expect him to call on you today. He has my permission to court you. I don't doubt he will propose. You must accept him. People have started talking about you. Lord Hennicker is the second most eligible young man of the Season. By turning him down, you have raised many eyebrows. You have also affronted his Mama who has a malicious tongue. You have comported yourself so well that the *ton* has forgiven the misdemeanor of your birth. But society is fickle. Any small indiscretion on your part and they will tear you apart and blame it on your tainted blood."

The interview left Lady Maria seething. Tainted blood, indeed! She felt her temper rise and her eyes took on a dangerous light. Gone was the Sweet Maria the *ton* worshiped!

Gwen was waiting for her. "What did her Grace want?"

"She wanted to remind me of my tainted blood! As if I can forget when she is forever reminding me of it!"

When Maria was sixteen, she had overheard the duchess bemoan the misfortune of her birth. "I don't know how that hussy trapped John. If not for her, I would not have to fear about Lady Maria's chances."

She didn't know what hurt more – the words or that the duchess refused to take her mother's name. She had wanted to go in and shame the duchess. Instead, she had chosen to show the duchess and her friends how much more lady-like a commoner's daughter could be.

"Come now, why did your grandmother want to see you?" Gwen asked.

"She wants me to accept Lord Daventon's offer."

"Lord Daventon? Have you met?"

"That is of no consequence. I shall accept the offer. It will keep Lord Hardwick away. And also ward off Lord Hennicker who will persist in his attentions if I remain unattached."

"What about Lord Daventon? What makes you think you will like him better than the rest?"

"I needn't like him in the least, Gwen. All I want is an engagement to last the Season."

Gwen was shocked that Maria meant to jilt Lord Daventon. It wasn't like her at all. She was never cruel. The duchess must have hurt her. Once she calmed down, she would see how wrong it was to betroth herself and not keep her word.

***

Maria thought it the perfect solution. She would drag on the engagement until she attained her majority and was legally free to snap her fingers at the duchess. She knew jilting Lord Daventon would create a scandal. So be it. Let the *ton* say she was her father's daughter! The duchess would disown her and the dratted family line would die out.

As Maria grew composed, she thought about Lord Daventon. She had never met him but knew he had an interest in Geometry. Two weeks ago, Lord Barrington came into the library, to borrow books for his wife. Maria was waiting for her turn. Lord Barrington glanced at the tome on Geometry in her hand. "Do you plan on reading it, Lady Maria?"

She had assured him that her pea-sized brain could not absorb anything from such a treatise. She wanted to use the geometrical designs in her embroidery.

Lord Barrington had rolled his eyes. "Not meant to be read. Could never understand it. No one reads such stuff. Except Daventon. Daventon reads everything! Never saw a fellow who could devour books like him. Doesn't look like a book reading fellow. Isn't either. Rows and rides. Best horseman. Have you met him, Lady Maria? Doesn't come up to London often."

"I'm not sure."

"He's a handsome fellow and has the bluest eyes you ever saw. Not easy to forget."

At that time she had thought Lord Daventon appeared to possess all the qualities she wanted in a husband. He was well-read, liked outdoor activities, and was handsome. But there was a flaw: he was a member of the *ton*.

Another pair of blue eyes came to her mind. Lord Barrington's companion had the bluest eyes she had seen and the most handsome face. He wasn't a member of the *ton*, either.

# Chapter 5

Lord Daventon's first waking thought was about the girl from the bonnet shop. What a pair of fine eyes she had! And none of the artifice and simpering that was a norm among young women of his class. She was natural and refreshing. She had promised that someone from the shop would call upon Lady Barrington. Would she come herself? The shop did not seem to have many employees.

Why was he thinking about her? Why couldn't he stop thinking about her? It was foolish. She was a lowly shop assistant. Moreover, he had decided to marry the duchess' granddaughter, and with his parents' history, he would be loyal to his wife. He may not love her or she him but for a marriage to stay alive, there had to be trust and loyalty. When parents feuded, the children took the brunt. He knew.

He had always believed he was not susceptible to female charms. He wasn't sure any longer that he was immune. Before he made a cake of himself over the maddeningly beautiful girl, he would call upon Lady

Severn's granddaughter. It was a necessary duty and the sooner performed the better.

Lord Barrington had loaned him his phaeton for the duration of his stay in London. Soon after breaking fast, he set off to Severn House but a few yards later, turned around and took the road to Lord Barrington's townhouse. He was helpless; he had to see if she was there. *"Fool! Imbecile!"* he scolded himself but his wayward heart pleaded with his reason, *"Only this one time."*

"Lord Barrington left an hour ago," the butler informed him.

"When is he expected back?"

The butler disappeared to inquire. "Lady Barrington will be pleased to receive you," he said, minutes later.

Amy looked upset and on the verge of tears. "Lord Daventon! Delighted to see you!" she murmured in broken accents.

"Lord Daventon sounds even more horrid than Lady Barrington. If I'm to call you Amy, you must call me Gareth."

"Gareth, it is not to be borne! You know I asked James for a bonnet from that delightful shop. He did not come home until after I went to bed. This morning he tried to hoax me with a bag of moonshine. I do not mind about the bonnet, I truly don't. I know James hates going into shops. But to tease me with odious falsehoods is the out and out of everything!"

"Amy, don't fly into the boughs. What did Barrington tell you?"

"He made up a story about both of you going to the shop at closing time where you met Mme. Brigitte who promised to come and see me this morning."

"Mme. Brigitte?"

"I knew he was bamming me! The wretch! I'll have his head for this!"

"Amy, we did meet a woman. I don't know if her name is Mme. Brigitte. She came out of the shop and we told her about you. She promised to send somebody today."

"Oh! So, it is true! I fear I misjudged him. I refused to believe him and he told me I was becoming a shrew and he did not know me any longer. If this is what London was doing to me, he said we had better return home. Gareth, how I wish you had come earlier. I would have known the truth and not driven James away. I fear he is very angry with me!"

"I am, Amy."

"James!" Lady Barrington shot out of the chaise and flung her arms around her husband's neck. He disengaged them and firmly held her away.

"I am angry, and hurt, and upset. I overheard you, Amy. You know Gareth for less than twenty-four hours but you are prepared to take his word. I spent an hour trying to convince you but you wouldn't believe me. That says a lot about your trust in me!"

His lady burst into tears. Gareth had an insight into what his friend had meant the previous day when he said he needed fresh air. He needed some, too, and stepped out of the door. A dark, closed carriage drew up and a young lad nimbly sprung out. As he started removing bandboxes from the carriage, Gareth asked, "Hasn't Mme. Brigitte come?"

The coachman, Adam, inquired what the matter was.

"Isn't Mme. Brigitte here? The young woman from the shop?"

Adam jumped down from his perch and faced Gareth. Crossing his arms over his barrel-like chest, he demanded, "Who?"

The boy piped in. "I think 'e means..."

Adam shut him up with a look and glared at Gareth. In a flash, Gareth understood he was trying to protect the young woman's identity. It made him absurdly happy.

"What young woman may that be?" Adam asked again without attempting the civility that a man of Gareth's obvious station demanded of him.

"How am I to know? Lady Barrington is expecting a woman from a shop. She's been talking about nothing else this morning. Where's the woman? I see she has sent the bonnets at least."

He beckoned the interested butler with a finger. "Show the boy in immediately. Don't waste time by sending him through the back entrance."

With a curt nod at Adam, he marched inside. Lady Barrington had stopped crying. On receiving the intelligence that a boy had brought bonnets for her to inspect, she sent for her maid. Lady Edwina sailed in at the precise moment, looking very fetching in a walking dress of embroidered muslin and a shepherdess-style straw bonnet. Her arrival was fortuitous; it freed Lord Barrington and Lord Daventon to seek the confines of the library.

"Gareth, you must not judge Amy harshly. She was never capricious. The physician tells me it is her condition that makes her so."

Suddenly, Gareth remembered his father lifting his mother out of the carriage and carrying her indoors. She was laughing. "Mama's not a baby!" he'd cried.

"She is, in her condition. We must keep her happy and comfortable."

Barrington did not notice his silence but continued to talk until Amy sent for them. She wanted Barrington's help, after all. She couldn't decide between three bonnets. Her husband solved the problem by coaxing her to buy them all.

On leaving his friends, Gareth decided he would visit the duchess on the morrow. He needed a ride to clear his head. A long ride, a ride that took him past the bonnet shop with its infuriating shut doors and blinds on the window.

***

Lady Maria rushed up to her room, the letter burning a hole in her pocket. Fortunately, she had got it before the duchess had checked the mail. Gwen was in the room, repairing a torn flounce on one of Lady Maria's gowns.

"Gwen! Mr. Stubbs has written!"

Gwen left off her work and shut the door. A week ago, Mr. Stubbs had advertised in the newspaper, offering to act for anyone who wanted to buy property in America. Lady Maria had wanted to meet him immediately. Gwen had dissuaded her from seeing him or writing to him in her own name. Lady Maria had written to him about buying the plantation that had belonged to her parents and signed the letter as Gwen Mathews.

With trembling fingers, Lady Maria tore open the envelope. "Gwen, Mr. Stubbs writes he can procure the plantation! As luck would have it, it is up for sale, though it may not remain so for long. He has enclosed a handbill about the plantation. Look!"

The handbill was a rough draft. It gave the address of the plantation, described it as a peaceful place, and had a smudged picture of the plantation.

"Is this my parent's plantation?"

"It could be," Gwen said slowly. "It looks like a plantation, and the color of the sky and the soil are indeed from that part of the world, but the house is not very distinct."

"Isn't it the same house?"

"I didn't say that. It looks a little different. This one is L-shaped. Of course, there could have been additions to it. The driveway looks the same."

"Mr. Stubbs writes he will be leaving London shortly, probably in three days. He has sent blank sale deeds and a copy of the power of attorney he holds. He will sign as soon as we pay the money. We can sail to America and get the deed registered, or he will do us the service, at a small fee. Gwen, if the plantation is sold to someone else, I may never be able to buy it back."

The plantation was Lady Maria's blind spot. In all other matters she was a woman of sense. Unlike other women of her class, she was practical, even shrewd. She ran her business profitably. She knew how to price the bonnets after considering the cost of material and labor, and shop rent.

"Gwen, I must show these papers to a lawyer. I cannot go to Pickwams, for they will inform her grace.

Do you know of any lawyer or anyone who has knowledge about legal matters?"

Gwen shook her head. Everything was happening very fast. She had to find a way to stop Maria from haring across to America.

"I have an idea! Remember the gentleman we saw with Lord Barrington? I suspect he is a lawyer. I saw him looking at us from the office of Meyers, Meyers and Meyers," Maria said.

"What was he doing with Lord Barrington?"

"Helping him on the delicate business of the bonnet. Lords always take help of lawyers when they are confronted with delicate business, you must know."

"Why did her grace send for you again?" Gwen asked, hoping to distract Lady Maria.

"The Earl of Daventon may call. She thinks he means to propose today itself."

"Why did you not tell me? I would have dressed your hair in a more becoming style. Never fear. He will wait. Gentlemen expect to be kept waiting."

"Gwen! Have you not been listening? There's no time to lose. We must go out immediately."

"But her grace..."

"We'll be back soon. This is important, Gwen. The earl can wait. Didn't you just say gentlemen expect to be kept waiting? Go and put on your outdoor things, that's a dear."

Lady Maria chose a bonnet to match the yellow muslin gown. She rummaged through a drawer and pulled out a scarf and a fringe of false hair. Packing it in a small bag with some more items, she called a maid and said, "Please inform her grace I'm going to the library. I'll be back soon."

She darted out of the door before the duchess could stop her. Gwen was waiting in the carriage. When they were safely on their way, Maria said, "Gwen, we must stop at the shop. I'll pick up some bonnets and send them over to Lady Barrington. I've met her twice and I know what will suit."

"My dear, Adam says you must shut the shop. I agree with him. It was different when Mme. Brigitte sold the bonnets through her friend. This Season you have let people know about the shop. Ladies are visiting it. If someone sees you there and questions Mme. Brigitte, she may betray you."

"The ladies can't see me because I sit in the small room with the one-way mirror; I can see them but they can't see me. And Mme. Brigitte thinks you own the shop but don't want people to know because of your reduced circumstances. I go there as your cousin and always dress the part. She can't know I'm Lady Maria because she doesn't go out into society. *Voila!* You and Adam don't have to worry!"

"Why are you doing this? The shop was making money without selling directly."

"This is more satisfying. I can transform a person. It's magical."

Lady Maria opened the bag she had brought with her and effected a quick disguise by putting on cheap gloves, a plain pelisse over her gown, and slightly scuffed shoes. Gwen fixed the fringe of false hair so that it covered half her forehead, and tied the scarf around her head. When she left the carriage, she looked like a young woman going to work in a shop or an upper-class house. Though her gown was rather fine, the unfashionable scarf and faded pelisse drew attention away from it.

They entered the shop through the side entrance to which no one else had a key. It opened into a small room which was out of bounds for Mme. Brigitte and the customers.

Lady Maria told Gwen which bonnets she wanted for Lady Barrington and Gwen went through the connecting door into the shop for them. Mme. Brigitte and her assistants were already in.

Mme. Brigitte looked harried. "Madame, we must hire two more women. The orders, they are increasing every-day! Thirty-seven new customers yesterday. I tell them they cannot have the bonnet for three weeks but they are pleased to wait. Lady Victoria North, she tells me to close the shop and she will open new shop for me in the Bond Street. She thinks I'm person who makes the beautiful design. She does not know it is you."

"And you do not know any better," Gwen thought. Mme. Brigitte was a lucky find. Her languid air did not encourage much talk. Her eyesight was bad and she could no longer do fine work but she could copy a design to a nicety and create a bonnet with a perfect fit. Moreover, she was an artist with a rare talent for sketching faces and could capture the features with a few quick strokes.

In fact, when Gwen discovered her talent and mentioned it to Maria, the idea of customized bonnets was born. The customers placed an order for the bonnet and gave their preference for the material on the understanding that Mme. Brigitte would select a bonnet that would suit them. They were free not to buy it but except in one case where the lady had an absurd liking for the color puce which became her not, the customers were more than happy with what they got. There was also the element of surprise. Like one giddy debutante waiting for her bonnet to be brought out gushed, "This is so exciting! I feel like I'm waiting for a surprise gift!"

Gwen arranged for the bonnets to be delivered to Lady Barrington. Because Tom, the delivery boy, would not be able to manage so many bandboxes, she requested Adam to take him in the carriage. It was a plain carriage. Nobody would recognize it. After spending a few more minutes with Mme. Brigitte, she came back to Lady Maria.

Lady Maria went through the sheaf of orders that had come in. As usual, Mme. Brigitte had neatly written down the measurements on the top of the page, followed by the color of the hair, eyes, complexion, age, and a quick sketch of the face. Lady Maria knew most of the women and had spent many an hour contemplating what would suit them best. It was easy enough to design for them. She made quick notes on the sheets, listing the type of bonnet, the trimmings and decorations, and the color of the gown it would complement the most.

Gwen grew restless. She feared they would miss the Earl of Daventon. "We should leave as soon as Adam brings the carriage. You can work on the designs at home."

"Gwen, I am keeping an eye on the offices of Meyers, Meyers, and Meyers. They appear to be a trifle crowded. I don't see Gareth either."

"Gareth?"

"The man who was with Lord Barrington last night. I suspect he works in the law office. He looked most comfortable at the window. I would prefer to consult with him. However, if I do not see him, we will go into the office before lunch."

Gwen was alarmed. It would not do to go into the office for it was often crowded and no place for a lady. But she knew that Lady Maria could not be swayed from her purpose when it was anything to do with her parents or the plantation. Yet, she tried. "Child, what of Lord Daventon?"

"The duchess wants him to wed me so she will contrive to keep him waiting."

***

Lord Daventon told himself he was there to see Meyers, Meyers, and Meyers on business. As he went up the stairs, he even managed to recollect a matter of reasonable importance.

"Mister! Mr. Gareth!"

It was she but she looked different. He would have taken her for a young woman come up from the country or an upper-class servant. Yet, she was the same. He would know those violet eyes and bow-shaped lips, and cream and roses complexion anywhere.

"I helped you last night about the bonnets. You must help me now. You work in the lawyer's office, don't you?'

Daventon did not correct her. He was drinking in her face with his eyes. She was a changeling but she was beautiful and vibrant and he had never been so stirred by any woman.

She touched his coat sleeve. "I saw you standing at the window yesterday morning. When I needed help with a legal matter, I thought about you immediately. Shall we go up? I want to speak about a confidential matter...sir". The sir was belated because Gareth's piercing blue eyes had made Maria forget the part she was playing.

Daventon remembered the small ante-room in the hallway. The clerk had requested him to wait in it. "There is a private room," he said.

"Capital! Gwen, let's go!"

Only then he noticed the young woman's companion. She looked disapproving. "My lady, you can't go into..."

"My lady?" he asked.

Lady Maria dimpled. "I told you my name is Milady, Milady Adam. It sounds like 'my lady' which is silly, isn't it? I work in a shop."

Daventon looked at her with narrowed eyes. Her accent was refined. The nobleman who had sired her had obviously taken care of her education.

Lady Maria read the suspicion in his eyes and adopted an ingratiating manner. "I heard Lord Barrington called you by your given name. I used it because I didn't know how to address you. What is your name, good sir?"

"Gareth Evenson," he answered glibly, Evenson being an obscure title he had inherited from an uncle.

Nat Stevenson was sitting behind a stack of files and daydreaming about the magnificent clothes he had the fortune of espying the previous night. He started when Gareth rapped a knuckle on his table.

"Mr. Meyers will not be in. He's attending court." On seeing Gareth, he sprang up from his seat and toppled the files to the floor.

Daventon waved Lady Maria and Gwen before him into the ante-room and shut the door. Lady Maria gave him the papers. "Sir, I want some advice. I want to buy a plantation in America. I c.came into some money."

"Miss, why do you not buy something in London? Maybe a shop of your own?"

"Sir, I want to start a new life in America. Have you never felt like leaving England and sailing away to a new land?"

Her eyes were fixed on his. In their depths, he saw an intense yearning, as if she did not ask the question idly and his answer held significance for her.

"It is of no import what I wish for. Too many ties bind me to England."

Lady Maria looked away, angry at her momentary weakness and her absurd desire to spend her life with a stranger. Giving herself a mental shake, she said brightly, "I must not take much of your time. Mr. Stubbs is prepared to sell me the plantation, er... a plantation in America. Will you please check the papers?"

Daventon was well-acquainted with legal matters. He scanned through the documents quickly.

"Miss Adam, the papers appear to be in order. However, as a measure of prudence, it will be better to arrange for a verification of land records. The power of attorney must also be verified and we must look into the antecedents of Mr. Stubbs. There are instances where crooks sell the land to more than one person. Mr. Stubbs may take the money and not register the sale. I would suggest you hand over the task of buying the plantation to a law firm."

Lady Maria's spirits fell. "Do these things take time? I don't want to wait."

"It can be months but it is safer to verify first. Miss, pardon the impertinence but I must speak my mind. America is no place for a young woman and running a plantation is by no means easy."

Lady Maria was devastated. What Gareth said about the papers made sense but she could not take a chance. If Mr. Stubbs was an honest businessman, she would be losing a rare opportunity. "Mr. Evenson, I must buy that plantation. It is a chance of a lifetime. Thank you for your time."

"I'll have someone make inquiries about Mr. Stubbs on your behalf. You work in the shop, don't you? I'll leave the report there."

Gwen, who was sitting in sulky silence, assessed Gareth. He was handsome and intelligent. If Maria chose him, she would drop her plan of sailing away to America. She might even convince him to sail with them. She knew Maria was determined not to wed anyone from the *ton*. It was better she married the handsome lawyer instead of jilting Lord Daventon and sailing away to an uncertain future.

"Please address the report to Gwen Mathews," Gwen said, surprising Gareth with a friendly smile as they left.

From the window, Gareth watched Lady Maria go across the lane and enter the shop. She must be down on her luck to wish to go to America. Even her shoes were scuffed. Unbidden, he thought of offering her his protection and chided himself for the thought.

He would not offer *carte blanche* to her or any other woman. He would visit Severn House on the morrow, and offer marriage to the duchess' stern-faced granddaughter.

# Chapter 6

"Mr. Evenson is right. We must not hurry with the purchase," Gwen said.

"Gwen, if Mr. Stubbs is a cheat, I will lose money but if he is honest, I'll lose an opportunity. We must go and see Mr. Stubbs."

"We must return home immediately. If her grace sends someone after you to the library, it will not do."

Lady Maria agreed. They returned to Severn House and found that the Earl of Daventon had not called in their absence.

Gwen decided she would find out more about the earl even though Lady Maria only wanted the engagement to be temporary. After fifteen years in England and accompanying Maria for four London Seasons, she had a mixed opinion about gentlemen of rank. While a few were men of honor, most were not worthy of a good woman. If she found Lord Daventon wanting, she would try to bring about a match between Maria and Mr. Evenson.

***

When Gareth returned to his rooms, a messenger from the physician was waiting. His heart beat fast as he broke open the seal. He heaved a shuddering sigh. The physician thought his mother's condition serious but not beyond repair. He permitted a visit and wrote that it could only do good.

He would go! Wrenrose was a mere two-hour ride from London. He would go and speak to his mother. It was long overdue. From his estates it was a good fourteen hours but distance had never been the issue. Since his father's death, a part of him had longed to visit his mother and to reclaim her but he felt she had rejected her children and was afraid of another rebuff.

None of that was important now. His mother could be dying and whether she loved them or not, he would not stand by and watch her waste away. The visit to the duchess would have to wait. He sent a note with his excuses and another to Lord Barrington who had invited him to spend the evening with him and Amy.

By late afternoon, he was on his way. Memories of his mother crowded his mind. Her soft voice and gentle touch made him impatient. It was as if he would never reach Wrenrose but when he drew up outside its gates, he felt he was not adequately prepared. Would his mother recognize him? Would she turn him away because he was his father's son? But he could not linger. A lackey was already hurrying to his side, to inquire his business.

"Lord Daventon, and you don't have to announce me."

The man's eyes glassed over. Daventon rode up the long curving driveway. The evening shadows had lengthened and he couldn't make out the house until he was almost upon it.

His coming caused a stir among the staff. He waived aside their ministrations and asked to see his mother. The housekeeper led him to his mother's rooms.

A nurse met them at the door. "My lord, your lady mother is asleep but she never sleeps for long. Would you like to wait by her side? You can call me when she's awake so that I may give her the cordial."

Gareth nodded and went in. The blinds were drawn close and the room was dimly lit. His mother was asleep. She looked lost in the enormous four-poster with its bolsters and high pillows. She slept like Laura, on her side and with her hand tucked under her face. He could make out her labored breathing. She looked a pale shadow of his memory of her.

On the table by the bed lay a book of Psalms and a chain with a heart shaped pendant. An old memory surfaced. He was ten, and standing outside his father's study. He heard every word his father said and the sobs that followed and would not abate in spite of Aunt Helena's soothing tone.

"Nell, I'm a fool. I cannot stay away from Catherine. Meyers told me she is ill and in Harrogate. I decided I would bury the past and bring her back. I need her, the children need her. But she has no need for us. She keeps his picture over her heart. I saw her open the turquoise pendant she was wearing and kiss it passionately. I wanted to tear it from her neck and stamp over it but he would still be in her heart! Why can't I forget her!"

He had run to his room, past the footmen and the maid polishing the silver, all of them shamelessly eavesdropping. He had made for the portrait of his mother in which she held Laura in her arms and he leaned against her chair. Her gown was blue, worn with a lace collar, and her ornament was a pearl necklace with a turquoise pendant. He grabbed the inkstand and hurled it at the portrait, aiming for the pendant.

When Aunt Nell found him an hour later, he was stony-faced. He did not shed tears for his mother after that. Over the years, he spent hours listening to his father turn maudlin over the love of his life but it did not bring memories of his mother. Aunt Nell thought he had forgotten her.

His long-suppressed jealousy burst open. For he had been jealous. The mother he adored and who had promised to love him and his sister forever loved someone else.

He was again the ten-year-old and he wanted to smash the pendant, for his own sake and for his father's. But as he looked at the frail woman on the bed, his anger seeped away. What was in the past had nothing to do with him. His mother had paid the price for her lapses. If she had been happy after leaving his father, it had not lasted, for sorrow and suffering were etched on her face.

She stirred and Daventon was at her side. He took her hand and held it against his cheek. She opened her eyes, and they were the same he remembered.

"Mother."

Lady Daventon tried to speak but a paroxysm of coughing overtook her. Daventon summoned the nurses. One of them prepared the cordial and the other adjusted the pillows while he raised her. He took the cordial from the nurse and brought it to Lady Daventon's lips, who, to the surprise of the nurses, sipped it meekly. After seeing to her comfort, the nurses left the room.

"How are you, Mother?" Daventon asked, shocked at how frail she had become; she was forty-four but looked much older.

Lady Daventon lifted a weak hand and Gareth held it between his own, willing his strength to flow into her. How fragile she was, her bones like those of a delicate bird, and her skin so pale, as if she had never been out in the sun.

"I'm glad you came before I left this world."

"Mother!"

"Do you remember what you were to call me when your father sent me away? Mama. You called me Mama and Laura said Ma-mma. That was the only word she knew. She called everyone Ma-mma; even you and your father were Ma-mma to her. She would walk to the table, toddler that she was, and point to something and say, Ma-mma. The plants, the flowers, the nurses were all Ma-mma. Did she look for me after I left?"

Lady Daventon began to cry weakly. When her sobs turned into a bout of coughing, Daventon gave her a draught of water and placed more cushions to support her.

"Mama, I don't know what happened between you and my father but he loved you to the end. We also love you and want you in our lives. Please come home."

"I cannot, Gareth, your father banished me.'

"He loved you. He would not wish you to suffer so. Do this for us, please. Let us forget the past."

***

Lady Daventon's condition started improving almost immediately. By the third day, she spent most of the time in the garden with her son, hanging on to his every word as he told her anecdotes about himself, Laura, and Aunt Nell.

Daventon penned a long missive to his aunt, telling her he hoped to persuade his mother to live with them, and his willingness to marry the duchess' granddaughter.

***

"Why do you look so serious, aunt? What tidings does my brother send?" Lady Laura asked.

Not wishing to raise Laura's hopes about meeting her mother until it was a reality, Lady Helena shared only the other significant news. "Nothing could be better! He writes that he saw Lady Maria at a bonnet shop and is certain she is the wife for him. I knew he would be smitten if he set his eyes on her. I hear she is exceptionally lovely."

Lady Laura wrinkled her brow, a habit she had when she was thinking seriously. "Aunt Nell, are you certain? Gareth does not want to marry a beauty because he does not want to fall in love. He has said that any number of times."

"Gentlemen will talk a lot of fustian until they meet their match. He must have fallen in love with Lady Maria at first sight. We must get him to buy a modish townhouse in London, and you can make your comeout next Season."

Leaving Laura to her thoughts and embroidery, Lady Harriet retreated to her room. She read the letter again. Though her brother, the late earl, and she had been very close, she didn't know the true nature of the breach between him and his wife. Whatever had transpired had destroyed him and Catherine. She had tried to save the children from the scars. She had succeeded with Laura but she attributed Gareth's cynicism to the trauma of his childhood.

He needed to heal as much as his mother and the sooner Lady Maria became his wife, the better. She wrote to the duchess, *"My nephew is smitten by your granddaughter. He saw her (of all places) outside a bonnet shop but did not speak to her as they were not introduced."*

# Chapter 7

"What does she want now?" Lady Maria demanded of Gwen's reflection in the mirror.

"Sit still, child, and let me do your hair," Gwen said, coaxing a long curl out of the chignon. "You must not keep her grace waiting."

"It cannot be about that marriage offer because Lord Daventon didn't call. Gwen, do you realize I haven't received a single offer during the last one week? I hope the Frenchmen don't leave anytime soon."

During the last week, Lady Maria's court had swelled with the inclusion of a party of French noblemen. This had caused her English suitors to close rank and leave no opportunity to make the Frenchmen feel unwelcome. The Frenchmen, in turn, were doing their utmost to make the English milords look unsophisticated.

At first Lady Maria was disgusted. "They remind me of the time when Lady Amelia walked into Hyde Park with a French poodle. It led to every single dog on the place barking his head off!"

Now she was happy that rivalry kept her suitors busy. This gave her ample time to think about her parent's plantation, and about Mr. Gareth Evenson. The report he had promised had not come. Mr. Stubbs also had not written. The plantation was most likely lost to her. Why had she put her trust in a stranger, however attractive he was? Why had she listened to Gwen? Even Gwen couldn't understand what the plantation meant to her.

"Do you like it?" Gwen asked, pulling Lady Maria out of her reverie.

"Thank you, Gwen. I suppose I must see her grace though she will put me in a bad humor with her talk of Scandal and Tainted Blood."

The duchess was in the morning room, seated in a winged chair beside the window, which was rather unusual. She always chose straight-backed chairs. She was also resting her feet on a footstool and held on to her cane, as if for additional support.

"I have received a missive from my dear friend, Lady Helena. She is Lord Daventon's aunt, you know."

Lady Maria gave a polite nod and waited. The duchess rubbed her forehead with a withered hand. Maria suddenly realized how much the duchess had aged. She was no longer the intimidating personage of her childhood but cut a rather vulnerable figure.

"I will not hide from you that I was anxious on Lord Daventon's account. He'd sent a note that family duty was taking him away from London but I had wondered about his intentions. It appears I misjudged him. Lady Helena writes that the earl is prepared to marry you. He saw you shopping in Bond Street and has written to his aunt that you will suit. He is coming to London this week and will call to make you an offer."

Lady Maria inclined her head but she was fuming. What kind of man took one look at a woman and decided to spend his life with her? He must be exceedingly shallow, and vain.

"Lady Maria, you do not look happy at the prospect. I am convinced you will like him. He is handsome and appears intelligent."

Lady Maria remained silent, holding herself aloof, and her demeanor was of one waiting to take leave.

The duchess sighed. "Lady Maria, you must learn to trust me. I am your friend. John was in all ways my son though I did not give birth to him. I owe it to him to see you well settled."

Lady Severn had never spoken to Maria about her parents. In fact, their conversations had never extended to anything beyond what was necessary.

"I owe a debt to John. Had he not come into my life, I would have led a solitary existence. Do you know I married the duke for John's sake?

"When I made my comeout, it was expected I would make a tolerably good match. I was never a beauty, being unfashionably tall, but my bloodline was impeccable and we had money. I was a romantic and yearned for a love match. I lost my heart to a silver-tongued impoverished count. My parents were livid. But I was madly in love and would have run off with him. Luckily, I overheard him ridiculing me to a friend. It shattered my heart but pride came to my rescue.

"I stayed through the Season. No one could guess I was heartbroken and disillusioned. Proposals continued unabated. My father and brothers could not make me accept any of them. I threatened to leave home and live on one of the properties, with an older relative as companion. Having a spinster daughter was the lesser evil.

"When I was twenty-eight, I met the Duke of Severn. He was thinking about marrying again. The dukedom needed a duchess. His mother invited me to their house party. John was but five. He was introduced to the guests and whisked away by his nurses."

Lady Maria leaned forward, no longer pretending disinterest.

"It was Christmas Eve. Snowflakes twirled in the air before falling gently to the ground. I slipped out of doors because I found parties oppressive. The same people met and tore into the latest scandal with an unseemly appetite. Not wanting to be found, I slipped into the maze. You know the maze is not a large one but it is certainly large enough for a five-year-old to lose himself in.

"John was sitting by himself on a seat. He knew he was lost but he was not crying. 'I ran away from nurse,' he said. 'I don't like her. I don't like nurses. I wish Mother was not dead.' He looked sad and lost, and close to catching a chill. I lifted him to my lap and held him close to me. He nestled in my arms and went to sleep.

"I had never held a child before. I did not know the healing magic children possess. I told my brother I would wed the duke if he would have me. The offer was made and we were wed. Everyone was happy because the match did credit to both our families."

Lady Severn grew silent. She had got a son, and John, a mother. She was sensible to her duties as the duchess. That was why the duke had married her, after all. She never gave him cause for complaint. If he noticed the time she spent with his son, he did not comment. When John went up to Eton, she kept up an active correspondence with him. She still had his letters. They were in a rosewood box, the first one tearstained, the childish scrawl heavily blotted. She followed his journey through Eton and Oxford, and looked forward to his holidays.

John, poor boy, was wary of coming home. His Grace kept him in the library for hours, talking to him about the Severns.

In another station of life, the duke would have been a meek man, a man who listened to opinions rather than air his own but he was the duke, and he felt the weight of his illustrious ancestors behind him. When he spoke, he heard the echo of their voices, and when he looked at the upright form of his son who bore the distinctive family nose and chin, he saw them in his face.

He wanted John to wed. For all the great deeds the family had performed, they were not a flourishing family. Every generation produced a single heir. His duchess, whom he had picked for her blue blood, presented him with a series of stillborn children after which the earl was born. She lingered a few hours after the birth and left her earthly life, her duty done.

So also was it with his mother. He was her only surviving child. He explained all this and more to the earl, who shocked him by saying the matter with the family was too much blue blood. Blood was supposed to be red, wasn't it? Then he left for the Continent with some friends. She suspected he left because the duke was putting him in an impossible situation.

"John met your mother and fell in love with her. He wrote to me. He said he was cutting his trip short and bringing Miss Janet Thornton to meet us. I was to speak to the duke and smooth matters for him. Unfortunately, his father had already selected the bride for him. Lady Theodosia was the daughter of a royal duke. The duke's missive about the match reached your father the day after he wrote to me. He knew his father would not go back on his word so he married your mother and brought her home.

"Matters spun out of control. They were both stubborn and would not listen. The duke threatened to disown John, hoping to bring him to his senses. John shrugged, and said, 'Sir, for once, don't play the duke!'

"He left. I could not believe he would leave me. I was his mother, his companion, the keeper of his secrets. I was the one he always turned to. So, I did what mothers have always done. I laid the blame on Janet's door. She had trapped him, enticed him away; my son was blameless. I wrote him a harsh letter and he did not reply. Then I sent him a wheedling letter, as if he was still a school boy, and he responded. He wrote he would not have anyone blame his wife. He was sensible to all that I had done for him but he had his pride; he would not return until the duke accepted his wife and presented her to polite society."

"He never returned?" Lady Maria asked.

"John wrote to the duke when you were born," the duchess answered, remembering that the duke had fumed at the birth of a girl, and blamed the commoner for not doing her duty. He had also faulted the three pages long letter which was all about the precious daughter. It was a most unmanly letter in the duke's eyes; it took too much notice of the offspring. A female offspring, at that! If it was a male, the duke would have brought him to England and petitioned for him to be made his heir.

Those were terrible days. When she tried to mend the breach, the duke blamed her. "You ruined him! You interfered when his tutor wanted to punish him for playing truant. You made excuses when he would not sit with me in the library and read about his ancestors. When his son is born, I will make him my heir. I will brook no interference from you, madam."

But no other child arrived to rekindle the duke's hopes. The worry and the port brought about a stroke. He recovered partially but with a new awareness of his mortality. He sent a representation to the parliament. He wanted to disown his son who was inept and had acted in a most dishonorable way. As there were no other male heirs, he appealed that in the event of his death, the duchess be empowered to run the dukedom and later if his granddaughter delivered a boy, he should be recognized as the duke.

It was a long shot but the family had money and clout, and a history of unparalleled service and monetary help to the crown. A month later, he died in his sleep. His lawyers located John in America. One of them, assuming he knew about the duke's representation, gave him the glad tidings that as the duke had passed on before the crown could take a decision about his strange request, he was the duke, and his ducal duties awaited him. To his surprise, his words infuriated John.

He had sent the men of law packing and written a blistering letter to her. "I will have nothing to do with an institution that makes men disown their own children. I am not the duke, or earl, or holder of any blasted antiquated title."

He had not attended the funeral or replied to Lady Severn's letters. As the business of the estate could not be kept on hold for ever, she had petitioned the crown. It was decided that she and later Lady Maria would be trustees, and Lady Maria's son would become the duke.

She knew John would not be pleased. She knew he was stubborn and would not want his daughter to be part of the family, and lineage. She had continued with the business of running the dukedom, and not given up hope of a reconciliation.

When Gwen and Maria arrived with the doctor's certificate about John's death, she was shattered. But a lifetime of training was behind her. She hid her emotions under a cold demeanor. She gave orders for Maria's care and the mourning, and shut herself in her room to mourn the son of her heart. Only her dresser and two upstairs maids knew she was prostrated with grief.

"Your grace?" Lady Maria murmured. She wanted to know more but Lady Severn had grown silent and was staring into the distance, a hint of tears in her eyes.

"Your father wrote about your birth but the duke did not forgive him. He died a bitter man. John refused to come home and fill his place though knowing John, it was grief and not anger that kept him away this time. I petitioned for running the duchy and holding it in trust for John, or his heir. John never came. You came, and the letter you carried brought the news about his demise."

Lady Severn did not add that she had shut herself away. Or had kept aloof because Maria had Janet's eyes and she could not bear to look at her.

"Maria, I am trying to do my best for you, for you are John's blood and my granddaughter. If you have not formed any other ties, I would urge you to this match. You may give me your answer after Lord Daventon calls on you."

Lady Maria took this as dismissal and returned to her room, where Gwen was waiting for her.

"Child, you look pale. What happened? Why did her grace want to see you?"

"Lord Daventon wants to make an offer. He saw me on the street and approves of me."

"Has her grace told you to accept? Is that why you look pale?"

"Her grace did not insist. She said Lord Daventon would call and I would most certainly like him."

Gwen's curiosity satisfied, Lady Maria tried to sort out her feelings. The duchess had reached out to her but she was not sure she wanted that.

# Chapter 8

Hyde Park and its environs were becoming more crowded than usual. More and more ladies of the *ton* were seen taking the air at the fashionable hour. Gentlemen thought it was their ardor, or perhaps the pleasant weather and the flowers in bloom, but it was Mme. Brigitte's bonnets. The ladies looked so fetching in them that they had to show themselves to the *beau monde*. While displaying their own charms, they did not fail to take note of what the other ladies wore. As a result, orders poured into the tiny shop. Ladies high in the instep shared space with ladies of lower rank on the sagging sofas. Dowagers who never spoke to tradesmen wheedled Mme. Brigitte and even her harried assistants.

None of this brought a smile to Lady Maria's face. "What ails you? You are not yourself." Gwen asked.

Lady Maria did not deny the charge. "Gwen, I do feel out of sorts. I wish the Season was over. I have started to feel positively old with so many fresh-faced debutantes making their comeout. They seem to be from the same mold, like freshly minted coins. I do not mean to hold myself up as any different. Rather, I have become the mold. I heard a mother tell her daughter she must emulate me, Sweet Maria, who is always amiable and who says the rights things."

"You don't have to accept Lord Daventon's offer, if that is troubling you."

"I don't intend to. The *bon ton* is not for me, and Lord Daventon is an epitome of the class. He has offered for me after seeing me in the street."

"He may have been smitten by you, love. You are far too lovely," Gwen answered.

"Even Lord Hennicker, who is not blessed with much sense, courted me for a week before proposing. Gwen, shall I send for Lord Hennicker and tell him I have reconsidered his proposal? He will by far make the better husband. But no, he has the most annoying laugh and he starts at every sound like an ill-bred horse. What shall I do?"

"Give Lord Daventon a fair chance."

"I'm afraid my mind is made up. I cannot marry a man who does not see beyond a pretty face. He must be a conceited boor or a fortune hunter, or worse. Oh Gwen! Why didn't you let me see Mr. Stubbs? We may have purchased the plantation and started a new life in America."

"Mr. Evenson hasn't sent the report about Mr. Stubbs. He didn't strike me as someone who would go back on his word."

"Did you like him, Gwen?" Lady Maria asked, and the look on her face told Gwen that *she* liked him exceedingly well.

Gwen decided it was time they did something about it. "My dear, shall I visit the lawyer's office and see Mr. Evenson?"

"Gwen, that's a good idea. Both of us will go."

Gwen did not protest. The outing would keep Lady Maria's mind off the ungallant earl. As usual, Lady Maria effected a quick disguise in the carriage. By the time they reached their destination, she looked like a very fetching shop girl.

"There are too many people about. I'll speak to Mr. Evenson and bring him to the carriage," Gwen said.

Lady Maria waited eagerly for Gareth. Her face felt hot and her heart started beating a little too fast. She hoped her color wasn't too high. In a few minutes, Gwen returned – alone.

"I do not understand it. There's no one by that name working in the office."

"Did you ask for Mr. Gareth Evenson?"

"I did. I also described him."

"How is that possible? I saw him standing at that window, looking out into the street. He also saw us in a private room"

"Do you think he may have been jesting with us? Men of a class do that with shop girls."

Lady Maria did not speak during the carriage ride home. As soon as she was back in her room, she took out her sketching book and said, "Gwen, I want to work on some designs."

Gwen left, shutting the door behind her. She also installed a footman outside the room, with instructions that my lady was not to be disturbed.

Maria made a neat curve on the paper. With practiced ease, she drew a bonnet and a face to go with it. The bonnet would suit a matron of advanced years, especially if she had a prominent jaw. Worn at a sedate angle, it would bring grace to a hard face. She sketched another bonnet, and a set of floral decorations. She worked with a steady hand and shut out the inexplicable pain of betrayal.

What did it matter that Mr. Evenson had played her for a fool? He was as perfidious as the men who courted her with flattery and flowers. Lord Daventon would be the same. He wanted a wife in name only while he dallied with shop girls and the like. She would teach him a lesson! She would become engaged and jilt him as soon as she attained her majority. She would lead him a merry dance and if she ever set eyes on Mr. Evenson, she would be hard pressed not to do him physical harm.

That very evening she spoke to Lady Severn. "Lord Daventon has done me a great honor. He has decided to accept me without knowing anything about me. I shall do the same. You may write to his aunt that I'm agreeable to the match."

"I expect he will call and offer."

"I shall accept. If other concerns continue to keep him away from London, you may write to his aunt. There couldn't be a better match. We are both Children of Scandal," Lady Maria said with some bitterness.

The duchess was speechless, and relieved. She did not press for answers or commend Lady Maria on making a wise choice. A lifetime of reserve stood between them.

Gwen tried to reason with her but Lady Maria shut her out. She would speak only of bonnets and the shop.

\*\*\*

Daventon called three days later. After the pleasantries were out of the way, the duchess said, in her blunt way, "My lord, I received a missive from your aunt. She tells me you have fixed upon Lady Maria as your choice. Please accept my felicitations."

Daventon was taken aback but murmured, "I shall be honored if Lady Maria will accept my suit."

"She already has. With both of you of one mind, we should make the necessary announcements. My secretary is very adept. Shall I tell him to send out a notification to the papers?"

"Your Grace, I had hoped to have a private word with Lady Maria today, with your permission."

"She is out shopping with a friend. She contrives to stay away from home during the morning."

At Daventon's look of surprise, her grace elaborated. "She has too many suitors. You may have heard of the proposals she has turned down. Some of those gentlemen will not take no for an answer and will continue to call. It has become rather embarrassing for her."

Daventon was surprised. When he had set eyes upon Lady Maria outside the bonnet shop, he had thought her a handsome woman with a regal bearing but certainly not a beauty. If she had persistent suitors, either stern looks were in fashion or her fortune was large.

"Of course, you would want to look into the settlements first. Lady Maria is heir to everything that is not entailed, and her son will inherit the title."

Daventon had no interest in the settlement. He was only looking for a wife who would take over the duties of countess and shepherd Laura through her Season. The week he had spent with his mother had made him believe more strongly that love was a quagmire. There was too much hurt involved. Apparently, Lady Maria also didn't believe in love; she wouldn't have agreed to the match without meeting him if she had romantic notions. They had that in common. They would lead an uncomplicated life of mutual respect.

He agreed for the engagement to be announced in the papers. That hurdle crossed, Lady Severn led the conversation to his family seat and her friendship with his grandmother. A quarter of an hour passed in polite talk and yet Lady Maria did not return.

"I have to take leave now. I will be leaving London in a day or two. My plans for the next month are uncertain. May I call on Lady Maria this evening?"

The duchess was suddenly afraid. Maria could be capricious. What if she changed her mind? It was better to have a *fait accompli* by having the engagement announced before they met. "I'm not sure. There are some invitations for this evening and for tomorrow. I tend to forget which ones we have accepted. I suppose that's due to my age. I'll send a footman around to let you know."

Daventon bowed over her hand and took leave. He was relieved rather than disappointed that he had not met his intended. He had discovered in the last few days that he was susceptible to a pretty face; the girl from the shop was never far from his thoughts. It was better he met Lady Maria after the engagement was announced when he had no opportunity of changing his mind.

Everything was working out for the best. His mother was coming back to live with him. He was engaged and would be married before the next Season so that his sister could have her comeout.

He drove to Meyers, Meyers, and Meyers. He had left instructions with them to make inquiries about a Mr. Stubbs who was dealing in properties across the Atlantic. Mr. Meyers was in and saw him immediately. "We ran a check on Stubbs. He is a shady character. We got the lowdown from another crook. He says Stubbs is a slippery customer and a master of disguise. He also goes by the names of Willie and Simpson."

"Your information is of the greatest import. I wish you had procured it earlier."

"Nat sent the report on the very next day."

It turned out that Nat had sent the report to his estate and not to Wrenrose as directed. Daventon took a copy of the report, put it in an envelope, and wrote, Gwen Mathews, all under the fascinated gaze of Nat who had never seen such an exalted personage perform so mundane a task.

Half a dozen carriages were lined outside the bonnet shop. The first one was a dark, plain carriage. He recognized it and the coachman. "You know Gwen Mathews, don't you? I saw you the other day. You also brought around the bonnets to Lord Barrington's. I want you to give this letter to her. It's very important you give it to her immediately. The person she is dealing with about property in America could be a crook."

"Guvnor, they have gone to meet him! Will they get into trouble?"

# Chapter 9

Lady Maria was not out shopping. Neither was she at the bonnet shop. That morning Mr. Stubbs had sent her another letter.

"Gwen! Mr. Stubbs is back in London. He writes he had gone to Bath to settle a deal. He will be at the same address for half a day. I can either see him today or wait for his letter after he reaches America. He is not certain this plantation will remain on the market for long but he promises to send me details about other properties."

Gwen was alarmed. She had hoped they had heard the last of Mr. Stubbs. She did not want her charge to buy the plantation. For two women, one of them a beauty, to start life alone on a plantation was nothing short of inviting trouble. Lady Maria had a better life here, and a greater chance of happiness.

"Gwen, we must see him and buy the plantation. You must draw the money. There is no time to lose."

The money from the shop was deposited by Gwen in a bank. To stall matters, she said it could be difficult to arrange for the withdrawal at such short notice.

"That is of no consequence. Bring my emeralds. We'll sell them or pawn them. I have always said I will use my own money to buy back the plantation but there is no time. We will pawn my jewels and you can withdraw the money and redeem them tomorrow."

"We can't do that! We'll stop at the bank. But something doesn't feel right about this offer. Mr. Stubbs sounds like a crook."

The letter had sent Maria into a tizzy. She wouldn't listen to anything. "We must meet him before deciding he is a crook. But we must seize this opportunity."

Gwen tried again. "The address is in an undesirable part of the city. It is unsafe to carry jewels or money."

"Adam will accompany us."

"Adam is getting old."

"We will take two footmen along."

"They will not keep it a secret and her grace will know."

"They will not tattle. I'll speak to them," Lady Maria said.

They set out a mere ten minutes before Lord Daventon called at Severn House. They stopped for Gwen to draw a substantial sum from the bank. Mr. Stubbs was at an address on a little known street. Adam, who wore a most ferocious frown, made some inquiries. The lane was not far from the street on which they had the bonnet shop. Adam drove to the bonnet shop and sent a footman to discover which alley led to the address.

Lady Maria and Gwen waited in the carriage. The footman, Ted, took his time coming back and received a mouthful from Adam. This led to an argument but before it could go further, Gwen intervened.

"Adam, you stay here with the carriage. Ted will lead the way, Lady Maria and I will follow him, and Joe, you will walk behind us."

Gwen poked Ted in the ribs as he stared at Lady Maria who was now dressed in a gown of grey calico, wore a flat bonnet with a false fringe of curls and a scarf over it.

Ted started off at a good pace. He walked up the street and turned into a narrow lane. A few yards further, he plunged into an alley.

"Are you sure this goes to The Hog?" Lady Maria asked, raising her scented handkerchief against the malodorous air.

"Yes, my lady," Ted said, and cheerfully dived into another serpentine passage.

They may have walked for not more than fifteen minutes but it felt like they were not in London. The street sounds were muted and, except for a few urchins and a drunk, the alleys were deserted.

"Here it is," Ted said, as they came out into a shabby square.

"Well done, Ted!" Lady Maria said, for it was no mean feat to have remembered so many twists and turns.

The Hog was at the corner of a dingy street. It was not precisely shady but the taproom was noisy and more than one man gathered behind them. The footman raised his voice and asked for Mr. Stubbs who lived above The Hog.

The man behind the scratched desk came out into the street. "You be meaning Mr. Stubbs?" he asked, all the time staring at Lady Maria and Gwen.

Ted pushed forward. "Mr. Stubbs it is."

"E's moved out."

"Has he sailed to America?" Lady Maria asked, and the man's eyes glassed over at the sight of the diamond ring she had forgotten to remove.

"Youse can find 'im in 'is office," the man said, and Ted took the directions.

Mr. Stubbs' office was not far away but it was not on the same street. Once again, they entered an alley. It was dark, narrow, and filled with the stench of decay.

Two men came from the opposite direction and blocked their way. Ted told them to stand to a side. One man made a coarse jest and leered at Lady Maria. The other pushed forward. A quarrel erupted and Joe rushed ahead to back up Ted.

As blows and curses were being exchanged, a third man crept into the alley behind them. He hit Gwen with something flat and heavy and snatched away her reticule.

"Run!" he shouted, and the two men who had started the altercation spun around and ran out of the alley.

"Ted! Joe! Go after them! No, stay. We should leave this alley before others come to rob us," Gwen said, rubbing her shoulder.

"Gwen, you are hurt?"

"My lady, it is of no consequence. We must walk on ahead."

The alley opened into another street with small tradesmen having their shops on it. It looked respectable.

"Gwen, how are you feeling? Shall we find a hackney and return home?"

Gwen knew Lady Maria wanted her parents' plantation above all things. It would be better to see Mr. Stubbs so that they did not have to seek him out again.

"Lady Maria, I am all right. Shall we see Mr. Stubbs?"

They found Mr. Stubbs at the address. It was a tiny office at the end of the street, with space enough to seat Mr. Stubbs and two visitors across a table covered with oilskin.

Mr. Stubbs was a big man in his thirties. After the innkeeper's sly looks and the thug's leer, his guileless blue eyes, ready smile and blond hair carefully combed over a bald patch were reassuring.

Gwen introduced herself. "I am Gwen Mathews. I wrote to you about the plantation."

Mr. Stubbs invited them to take a seat. "These are cramped quarters. But then, this is England. My office in America is spacious. I can't wait to get back. Have you come to sign the papers? That is wise. You will not get such a bargain again."

"I am afraid we will need time. We were bringing the money but were set upon by thieves. They snatched away my reticule."

"Ladies! This is shocking! I wish I was staying for a few more days so that I could give you time to make other arrangements. Unfortunately, I sail tomorrow."

"When do you sail?" Lady Maria asked, and in her agitation, forgot to disguise her speech.

Mr. Stubbs had already noticed the diamond ring and the pampered hands that could not belong to a woman of the working class. In a trice, he knew the truth. She was the one who wanted the property and she had money. He had already guessed there was sentiment behind the purchase. The property must have belonged to a family member or a loved one. He had, in fact, planned a charade on that hunch.

He drew out a picture from the file in front of him. It showed a grassy mound with a roughly hewn wooden cross. "There is a grave on the plantation. Is this why you want it?"

Before Lady Maria could touch the picture, he put it back in the file. Involuntarily, she clasped her hands. Stubbs knew the bird was snared.

"When do you sail?" Lady Maria asked again.

"I sail tomorrow but today is the last day I can do business with you. I forget. Business is a dirty word in England but you must forgive me, I am American. Tomorrow I shall be busy taking leave of close friends. Dear ladies, my heart bleeds for you but I can't help."

"You will have to give us time. A friend could act for you, perhaps?" Gwen asked, remembering vaguely that deeds could be done by representation.

But Lady Maria would not have it that way. She was as helpless as a rabbit hypnotized by a snake. She couldn't let the opportunity slip past her.

"We shall sign the papers today. We will be back in two hours," she said.

Stubbs cleared his throat. "Dear lady, I have given you a week. I cannot give you more time without an assurance of sale. If you change your mind, I will not be able to sell this excellent plantation before sailing. You must make some payment."

The man did not trust her word! Lady Maria couldn't believe the vile insult. She jerked up her head, and in that moment glimpsed the thugs who had attacked them in the alley. They were standing behind a carriage across the street and looking at the shop.

Suddenly everything fell into place. Stubb's office was on a street but he had directed them to the inn. He knew they would come with money and he had sent the men to rob them.

"My good man, we have been robbed. How do you expect us to make payment?" Gwen demanded.

"You can leave a valuable. I will accept the ring."

Lady Maria stood up. "We will not be buying the plantation," she said, her voice quivering with rage, and propelled Gwen out into the street, trying to think what they must do. Further thought was abandoned as their carriage came clattering down the street. Before Adam could still the horses, Mr. Evenson jumped out!

"Did you come here about purchasing the property?" he asked urgently. "Have you paid Stubbs? I believe he is a blackguard and he dupes people."

"We didn't pay him because we were robbed," Gwen said.

Lady Maria found her voice. "He sent the men to rob us. He's inside."

Daventon kicked open the door and rushed into the room. It was empty. He rushed to the sole window and looked out. It was a sheer drop from the window to a pile of garbage and Stubbs was nowhere in sight.

"He's escaped!"

"The men who robbed us were behind that carriage minutes ago!" Lady Maria said, and Ted and Joe ran down the street looking for them. Adam also followed. Daventon went behind the shop, to look for Stubbs.

"When did you see the men?" Gwen asked.

"Just before he asked for my ring," Lady Maria answered, looking shattered. Was the plantation for sale or had he lied? And the picture that had made her lose her head? Was it real? She had yearned to possess the home her parents had made, and it had turned out to be a lie.

Daventon returned and misunderstood her pallor. The poor girl had lost all her money. It may not be a very big amount but she had inherited it and it must have amounted to a nest egg. It was his fault. She had come to him for help, she had trusted him, a virtual stranger, and he had let her down.

"I was away from town, and Meyers did not forward the report to my address. I returned today and went to see him. He told me Stubbs is a crook."

"Away from town? We thought you worked in the law office," Gwen said.

"I am sorry if I gave that impression. I have…dealings at the office and tend to make myself at home."

Lady Maria's despondency fell away like a cloak. Her heart sang, her eyes shone. Mr. Evenson had not lied! He had not played a jest on her. He was true and honorable. Though he thought her a mere shop girl, he had gone to the trouble of helping her.

Daventon's gaze locked with hers. How enchanting she was! Her eyes were clear yet held secrets, secrets he could read, and they were the same as his. In that instant he knew Milady had spent the hours thinking about him. Like him, she had felt a connection which she had not denied. Her parted lips spoke of want and need, a need he felt as keenly as her. Her face was his mirror just as she was his reflection.

Lady Maria was lost in the mesmerizing blue eyes. She gazed into them and yet she was aware of the rest of him. The planes of his face, the cleft in his chin, his hair unfashionably short but with a tendency to curl, and a smile hovering around his mouth, in which there was wonder, and joy.

Gwen was alarmed. Adam and the footmen would be back any moment. While Joe and Ted were not very observant, Adam would throw a fit. He was devoted to Lady Maria for her own sake and for her father's. He chaffed at having to conceal her activities. If he found her standing in the middle of the street, her face inches away from a gentleman's, he would not hesitate to speak to the duchess.

"Mr. Evenson!" Gwen said rather loudly, and prodded him.

Daventon blinked, as if waking up, and stepped back hurriedly. Lady Maria blushed an enchanting shade of pink which once again drew his eyes to her but Gwen was determined in getting his attention.

"What else did you learn about Stubbs?" she asked.

"Huh?"

"What did you find out about Stubbs?"

Daventon ran a hand over his face, as if clearing away the enchantment, and said, "He operates under different names and uses disguises. He is too quick for the authorities. As complaints start coming in, he changes his name, appearance, and the way he cons people."

"He has blue eyes, blond hair, a bald patch," Lady Maria offered.

"His teeth are very white and one tooth is of gold. He was wearing a thick silver ring, with a blue stone," Gwen added.

"The hair, the gold tooth, and the ring could be for the disguise because those are the things most people would notice first."

"He looked tall, almost as tall as you," Lady Maria said, throwing an appreciative glance at Daventon.

"Did you see his shoes? He may have added a few inches to the shoes. Anyway, we can only make a report to the authorities. The rest is up to them. Do you want my assistance in filing a report about the robbery?"

"No!" Lady Maria squeaked, "I mean, we don't need help."

Gwen came to the rescue. "My...my brother will see to it. He is the coachman who brought you here. Our mistress doesn't mind if he uses the carriage when she does not engage it."

There was nothing left to do except to take leave, Daventon realized. He wished he could at least shake hands but that would be improper so he tipped his hat in their direction and hailed a hackney.

Lady Maria followed him with her eyes, willing him to turn. But she had no way of knowing whether he did; a carriage blocked him from view.

During the ride back home, Gwen left Lady Maria to her thoughts. She could divine they were about the handsome Mr. Evenson.

Lady Maria spent most of the day in her room, singing snatches of songs, and sketching cheerful caps and bonnets. When Gwen came to help her get ready for bed, she danced with her around the room, laughing all the time. Gwen had never seen her happier. She was reminded of Maria as a child, laughing as her father lifted her high up in the air.

The next morning, the maid, Rosie, came into Maria's room before Maria was fully awake. She bobbed a curtsy and giggled.

"What now, Rosie?" Lady Maria asked. She liked the maid though everyone thought her silly; she was either giggling or having the vapors.

"My lady, I came to wish you very happy. He is very handsome."

Lady Maria bolted out of bed. Did everyone know about Mr. Evenson? Had she told all in her sleep?

"Her grace wants you down soon. She is expecting callers what with the engagement in the papers."

"Engagement? My engagement? With whom?"

Rosie thought it was a fine jest and went into peals of laughter. "With Lord Daventon! It is in the papers!"

Gwen rushed in, looking worried. She sent Rosie away and held up the newspaper sheet. "This says you are engaged to Lord Daventon. Her grace's secretary must have blundered. He is always in a tearing hurry."

"I told her grace I would wed Lord Daventon if he made an offer. He must have offered," Lady Maria said.

"But that's not right! You haven't even seen each other!"

"He has seen me in the street and has decided I will suit. I don't need to see him because I know he will not suit."

"Child, do you mean to wed him?" Gwen asked, trying to understand.

"No, Gwen. I do not."

"What are you saying? Why did you agree to the engagement if you mean to break it? There will be a scandal."

"Don't forget I am a Child of Scandal and carry tainted blood. The *ton* will not be surprised," Lady Maria answered, trying to sound nonchalant.

In truth, she was feeling overset by the turn of events. It was all too sudden, and real, and she had no idea how to wriggle out of the impossible situation.

# Chapter 10

Daventon declined Lord Barrington's invitation and dined at the club. Later, he sat by himself nursing a glass of mediocre port.

"Milady! My lady!" he murmured, not able to stop thinking about the day's encounter. Was it love, or the lust that drove men to ruin? He had never experienced anything like that. Whatever it was, he would have to forget about it. If she was an eligible young lady, he would have thrown aside his resolve of not marrying for love; that would have been an easy thing to do.

But Milady was not for him. Any attachment, except of a sordid nature, would lead to scandal, and it would destroy Laura's chances even before she made her bow to Polite Society. A mother of questionable character and a brother who was sunk low by marrying a commoner would make it impossible for her to hold up her head. She did not deserve it. Neither did Aunt Nell.

He would not see Milady again. Fortunately, he did not know anything about her except that she worked in the bonnet shop. He would even stop thinking about her.

When he could.

The next morning, Lord Barrington sent around a footman to the club, asking Daventon to breakfast with him and Amy. As soon as he entered the house, Amy welcomed him with a volley of questions. "Why didn't you tell us you were courting Lady Maria? When did you offer for her? I find her most amiable, and she possesses impeccable taste!"

"Our felicitations, Gareth," Lord Barrington said, beaming.

So the duchess had sent out the notice, Daventon thought, dismayed and relieved at the same time.

"You have been noticeably absent. How did you meet Lady Maria?" Lord Barrington asked.

"The match was arranged by the duchess and Aunt Nell," Gareth said, sidestepping the question. He also parried Amy's questions without hurting her romantic notions and retreated into the library with Lord Barrington.

"You have made quite a match but don't look happy. Does the scandal in Lady Maria's family bother you?" Lord Barrington asked bluntly.

"James, I have lived with scandal. In fact, Lady Maria and I may possibly have only that in common between us."

"You may have love," James said. "Husbands may fall in love with their wives. It is not expected but it is possible."

Daventon shrugged and changed the topic. "My mother's physician has given a good report. He is hopeful she will regain her strength if she is kept engaged and happy. She has agreed to come and live with me. I have decided to spend as many days as possible at Wrenrose. If her recovery is slow, I shall send for Laura and my aunt to join us."

"Amy will be disappointed you are leaving London. She was hoping for visits from you and Lady Maria. She admires her very much and would like it above anything if she would call."

Daventon found it difficult to believe that Amy had anything in common with Lady Maria. But then, he did not know his intended, and appearances were often deceptive.

"The Mayricks have their family seat a few miles from Wrenrose. The dowager countess is holding a house party next week. Amy wants to attend. The physician has said she may travel the short distance if the carriage is well sprung. As the Mayricks are close relations and the party will be a dull affair, I've decided to take Amy. The country air will do her good and she will not yearn for gaiety because there is none to be had."

"How can you say the party will be dull?" Gareth asked, curious.

"Lady Mayrick only invites guests who are married or engaged. She refuses to invite unattached people, not even spinsters or widows under the age of fifty. She says there is enough tomfoolery during the Season. While she has nothing against people trying to make a match, there are others who need a respite from the marriage mart. She hosted the first party six years ago and you know the *ton*, they took it up as a novelty. Now everyone who has no unattached relative looks forward to the 'blessed dullness' of the Mayrick house party. There is nothing to do there, no card tables are laid out, and no music is forced upon the guests. The guests are left to their own devices between meals. Some read, others go for walks, or play a hand of whist."

"Bring Amy to Wrenrose when you are there," Daventon said.

"I don't know. That stretch of road is rather bad and will jostle a carriage. You must come instead. I'm sure you will receive an invitation."

Daventon nodded. If his mother was improving and wanted to start going out into Society, the Mayrick's party was just the place.

That very afternoon he left for Wrenrose. Needless to say, he took the circuitous road and felt a pang of disappointment at not seeing Milady. When he reached the estate, his mother had made the effort to have the drawing room opened and the dust covers off the furniture and frames. She ordered tea and scones to be brought in and fussed over him while he ate, sending for another pot of tea when he mentioned a blend he liked.

Lady Daventon was delighted to hear about the engagement. She thought it was a love match. When Daventon told her it had been arranged by Lady Helena, she asked, "Is Lady Maria happy with the choice made for her? I don't want you to suffer a fate similar to mine."

*I do not want to suffer a fate similar to my father's,* Gareth wanted to say but held his peace; Lady Daventon was only now recovering and he would not do anything to upset her. Her behavior baffled him. He could not doubt that she loved him and Laura, and had also loved the earl, and yet, she had left them for another man. Who was he? Had he spurned her love?

She continually asked about Laura. She couldn't decide whether she should send for her. "She must hate me so much."

"Laura is like you, Mother. She is incapable of hate. She doesn't know much about you but you are her mother and she loves you. She also looks like you. She has your height and your coloring."

"I want to see her, Gareth, but ..."

"You need time. Why don't we first try to make you feel yourself? I'm happy to see you out of bed. The housekeeper told me you have seen to the arranging of the meals, which you have never done before. Flanders always saw to everything."

"I never had an incentive, Gareth. A woman needs a family. I used to plan elaborate meals when we entertained, and wholesome picnics which you loved. After all that, I didn't have the heart to do anything. I would have gone into a decline had Flanders not coerced me into taking my meals and a daily constitutional. Do you remember her? Of course, you do. She didn't let me engage a nurse for you; she said she would look after you. It would be like looking after me again. Poor Flanders! She was devoted to me. I fear the events broke her heart."

Daventon sat beside his mother, one arm loosely draped over the back of the sofa, his hand grasping her agitated fingers. He let her speak on, inserting a word here and there, placing them strategically so that the conversation often turned to Laura. His mother was always happy to talk about Laura.

"Gareth, my jewels are all locked up safely in my bedroom. Your father sent them after me but I never wore them. The pearls and sapphires will be just the thing for Laura. I have a gown of the finest lace. There are others too, all of them barely worn. Flanders had put them away in a rosewood chest. They are very pretty. Is Laura slender like me? But what am I thinking! The gowns would be outmoded."

In spite of her animation and her eagerness to look after Gareth, she tired easily. But getting tired was better than wasting away in a dark room, so he let her recount incidents from his childhood.

For all the time he spent with his mother and also attended the post that was being forwarded to Wrenrose, he could not stop thinking about Milady.

"Are you thinking about Lady Maria?" his mother asked one afternoon, as he sat with her in the rose arbor.

"No."

"I thought not. You never mention Lady Maria. Who is she, Gareth? I do not mean to pry but I find you often distracted. Who is the woman who has captivated you? If your heart is engaged elsewhere, you cannot hope to find happiness with Lady Maria."

"There is more to life than pursuing one's heart's desire. There is duty to family, and name," Gareth said, and watched the joy drain from his mother's face.

Immediately, he was contrite. "I am sorry. I didn't mean to pass judgment. Your life is your own. Whatever happened may have blighted my father's happiness and left me and Laura without a mother but I want to put the past behind us."

Lady Daventon made to speak and thought the better of it. She patted Gareth's hand and chose to talk about the roses instead.

\*\*\*

In London, Lady Maria also made polite conversation about the roses in bloom, the weather, and fashion with the numerous callers to Severn House. They came to offer their felicitations and to look for scandal. For there must be a scandal. No one had seen Lady Maria with Lord Daventon. What had brought about this hasty engagement? Some sly matrons wanted to know if the date was set, to find out whether the marriage was an act of expediency.

The duchess let it be known that though the engagement was newly announced, an understanding had existed between the families. The information was little more than a crumb and it did not satisfy the gossips. The most vicious of them all was Lady Goodall. She thrived on tearing reputations and had long looked for a way to bring Lady Maria down from her pedestal.

She leaned forward and in a conspiratorial tone meant to be overheard, said, "Your grace, Lady Maria is all that is good and kind. I cannot help but be concerned about her. She will be aligning herself to the Daventon name, and the Scandal will taint her as well."

Lady Maria was about to make her entrance. She overheard Lady Goodall and paused at the door.

"Lady Goodall, I thank you for your concern but I must follow my own counsel. Lord Daventon is a good match for Lady Maria."

Lady Goodall raised her nasal voice a notch. "I thought it my duty, as we have known each other for ever so long. Lady Maria's mother was…"

"A lady," said the duchess, daring her to speak another word.

In the silence that followed, she continued, "Lady Maria's mother was an American and though not of noble birth, possessed qualities of a true lady. Birth alone does not make a lady. Don't we all know women of noble lineage who do not possess a shred of decency or dignity? It has been a matter of profound sorrow to me that the duke set the family name above everything else. Lady Maria's mother, Janet, would have made an excellent duchess. I'm persuaded she had qualities to endear herself to all of us. You have only to look at Lady Maria! When she came from America, she was but six and yet, despite her youthful years she possessed excellent manners. I credit her mother for her conduct because she reared her."

Tears blurred Lady Maria's eyes. Turning back, she rushed up the flight of stairs, startling the footman hovering in the passage. The duchess had defended her mother! She had mentioned her by name, and had delivered Lady Goodall a stinging set down.

An alarming thought came to her. Would the engagement reopen the old scandal? Like Lady Goodall, would others rake up the past and speak ill about her mother?

Lady Severn had spoken up but that could start another set of rumors; Lady Goodall would see to that. She had to do something. The *ton* paid as much attention to scandal as to dress, and if the dress was in a new fashion, it took precedence.

She sent for Gwen. "I shall wear the new gown made to mine own design."

Half an hour later, she went into the drawing room. She was dressed in a high-waisted gown, the cotton fabric lightly embroidered with silk thread, the square neckline and the puffed sleeves edged with sawtooth trim and tiny beads. Panels instead of pleats flared from the waist. Her overdress was of fine muslin and was embroidered in the same tones as the dress.

She wore a bandeau above the cluster of artfully arranged curls. It had embroidery to match her gown.

As the callers felicitated her, they stole glances at her gown. Some gawked at her bandeau and the conversation turned to fashion. Were bandeaus making a comeback? What about beads?

In the coming days they continued to be besieged by callers. The reason was an aura of mystery surrounded the engagement. No one had seen Lord Daventon court Lady Maria. Though the engagement was announced, he did not number among the morning callers. He hadn't taken up Lady Maria in his curricle to Hyde Park, or promenaded with her during the fashionable hour.

The duchess sat through the visits though they fatigued her. Her dresser grew worried and shared her concern with Gwen.

"We can leave London. Lady Maria will not mind missing the rest of the Season," Gwen suggested.

"If we return home, it will lead to unnecessary speculation. Her grace will not agree to anything that will cause gossip about the match."

Even after fifteen years in England, Gwen found it surprising how scared the rich and powerful were of gossip. They had so many privileges but could not enjoy them. Their servants were more free and often happier than them.

"How about a trip to another place? That should not cause gossip," she said.

Her grace liked the idea when her dresser suggested it. "But where? Bath is always an option but..."

"It's not the same as before, your grace," her dresser inserted smoothly, knowing well her mistress had started to find long journeys exhausting. "How about the Mayrick's house party, your grace? An invitation came in as soon as Lady Maria's engagement was announced," she asked.

***

When Lady Maria came down for breakfast the next morning, the duchess was already at the table. She dropped a curtsy and took the chair opposite her.

"You look delightful, my dear," the duchess said, inexplicably wishing that Lady Maria had given her a kiss instead of a curtsy.

She was certainly getting maudlin in her old age. It was enough the coldness between them had thawed. The days when she had turned away from the lonely child, and the years when she had watched her from behind curtained casements not knowing how to speak to her, or even whether she wanted to speak to her, were in the past. Now she joined Lady Maria for breakfast though all she wanted was tea and toast.

"It's a sunny morning," she said, as a footman removed the covers.

"We can expect callers raining on us," Lady Maria said, knitting her brow prettily.

"You handle them well. Even Lady Goodall forgets to dredge up gossip when you are present."

Lady Maria smiled. Fashion did rule over gossip.

"We could leave London," her duchess remarked.

Lady Maria's cup remained suspended for a fraction of a minute.

"We can't go back home without hosting an engagement ball. How about a week in the country? Lady Mayrick has sent an invitation for her house party. It has earned a reputation for restful dullness. We might find that pleasant."

Lady Maria made a moue. She no longer wore her polite mask and that delighted her grace. The gel was accepting her!

It was soon decided they would attend the house party. Leaving her grace to send the acceptance, Lady Maria went back to her room, to prepare for the morning callers. Gwen noticed that she looked preoccupied with her thoughts.

When she learned about the proposed visit, she asked, "Are you anxious about the shop? The party is only for a week. I heard that most guests don't stay that long. The servants must be having a difficult time, not knowing how many will sit for dinner."

"What about the hostess? How does she seat her guests?" Lady Maria asked, diverted.

"I don't know."

She lapsed into silence.

"Is it the shop?" Gwen asked again.

"Mrs. Brigitte has copies of all my designs. She will tell customers she has stopped making new designs for the Season, and they must choose from the portfolio.

While she has no talent for creating new designs, she has taste and will be able to suggest what will suit."

Gwen left her alone after that. Lady Maria was indeed unhappy about leaving London. At first she had thought her grace wanted them to go home. Go home and never see Gareth again! She had almost dropped her teacup.

She knew she was being foolish. How could she find Gareth? He didn't work at Meyers, Meyers, and Meyers. She knew nothing about him. He must be living in London but he could as well be on another planet; he was not a member of the *ton*, their paths were not likely to cross.

He had looked at her as if she was everything to him. How her heart had soared. This is love! I'm in love and Gareth loves me, she had thought. She wasn't so sure now. Gareth hadn't tried to meet her. It would be the easiest thing to leave a message at the shop, and to arrange a meeting.

Lady Maria was also troubled by her engagement. In the beginning she had felt contempt for the earl and thought him ragged mannered not to care to speak to her before offering. It was better this way, she had thought. Her conscience would not assail her when she jilted him.

Now she wondered whether there was more to the engagement. Was Lord Daventon a proud man who felt his mother's scandal keenly? Had he offered for her because he did not want to risk refusal from other debutantes who came from unblemished families? Some of the callers who knew him felicitated her with sincerity, telling her she had made a good choice.

The Stubbs episode also preyed on her mind. It was not the loss of money, she could earn it over through her bonnets, it was the loss of hope. She realized the plantation was someone's home, and she might never be able to buy it.

There was the duchess' overture of friendship. Lady Maria had built her life on the resentment she felt for the duke and the duchess. They had denied her parents, so she would deny them. The *ton* thought her mother lowborn and vulgar; she would show the *ton* what it was to possess grace and impeccable manners. When matrons held her up as an example of poise and beauty, extolling their charges to emulate her, she felt as if she was upholding her mother's name.

It was her crusade against the duchess and the *ton*, and it sprang from her childhood hurts and was therefore childish. She had wanted to prove herself to the ton. She had never cared for their homage, and considered it of scant worth. They deserved her scorn as they were incapable of love.

Now she knew Lady Severn had loved her father like a son. She had grieved for his death. She hadn't banished him from her heart. Neither had the duke. They were wrong but they had suffered, and Lady Severn was trying to reach out to her, seeking her beloved John in his daughter.

What was she to do? Her childhood memories of a cold woman who refused to look at her would not let her love the duchess but could she forgive her? What about Lord Daventon? If he was a good man, would she be doing him an injustice? And Gareth? Gareth loved her but did not want to marry her, perhaps because he supposed her to be a lowly shop girl. If he could deny his love for social reasons, he was no better than Lord Daventon and the *ton*.

The Mayrick's party looked inviting. She would find solitude to sort out her thoughts.

# Chapter 11

The duchess and her party left for Mayrick Manor a day later. Once they left the confines of London, the journey became pleasant.

It was a sunny day, with a gentle breeze. Lady Maria usually traveled in a separate carriage with Gwen, but this time she was with her grace who seemed determined to sit through the journey. Her dresser and Gwen were also in the carriage. The conversation was mostly about Maria's father. Then, to Maria's immense delight, her grace asked Gwen about their home in America.

"Mr. Marvel, I mean, his lordship was popular with everyone. He didn't say much about his life in England but I once heard him say he wished he had a miniature of you and the duke. He wanted a likeness painted, for Mary to know her grandparents. Mr. Marvel and the missus were very attached to each other, your grace, and they were happy."

The journey was well spent in reminisces and Mayrick Manor arrived too soon. Lady Mayrick received them graciously. They were shown to their rooms, with the option of coming down to tea or having a tray sent up. The duchess chose the latter.

When Lady Maria came down for tea, there weren't many guests in the drawing room. Her hostess explained, "Tea is also served in the library and on the lawn. Would you like to have it there? Or keep us company in here?"

The 'us' comprised of Lady Mayrick, Lady Havisham who was deaf in one ear and carried a trumpet, and Lord Turner who was famous for dribbling snuff on his overcoats, in addition to being deaf in both ears.

A young lady dressed in the height of fashion entered. The cut and the color of her dress proclaimed she was a married lady, though the wide-eyed gaze and the rather tremulous smile betrayed her youth and inexperience.

"Amy, my dear! Come in. Are you sufficiently rested? Come and meet Lady Maria. Lady Maria, this is Lady Barrington. Her delicate condition has kept her away from the gaieties of the Season."

Lady Barrington threw a startled glance at Lord Turner and blushed.

"Never mind him, my dear. He's deaf as a post. Come and have your tea. You young ladies can entertain each other while I see to the guests in the library."

"I remember you, Lady Barrington. We met at the library when you were just come," Lady Maria said as they made their bows to each other.

In no time Amy forgot her bashfulness and was talking nineteen to a dozen. "You must think me absurd, dressed to the nines in the country!"

"You look very charming, Lady Barrington. The sarsenet overdress becomes you. Not many can carry that shade of yellow, I can tell you that."

Lady Barrington clasped her hands to her breast. "You are so kind, Lady Maria. You see, I know I'm overdressed but I've got heaps of gowns I haven't worn and soon I shall not be able to fit into them!" And with this, Amy poured out her woes. Soon they were using first names. Amy was a talker, and it suited Lady Maria.

"Shall we walk in the garden? My physician tells me I can start taking a little exercise."

"Then you should. Do you need a shawl? It will get a little cold if we stay out late."

"I don't want to cover this gown with a shawl. And I want to take a walk because I have a very pretty new bonnet. It's made by the woman who creates yours. I don't have the opportunity to wear it to Hyde Park so I shall wear it here and hope the geese in the park forget to cackle when they see it and the ducks in the pond stop and stare!"

Lady Barrington's maid brought the bonnet from the bedroom. Lady Maria groaned inwardly. The bonnet clashed horribly with the gown. It would kill the yellow sarsenet and die in the process.

"Are you sure you got the bonnet from the same shop? I have a similar one and Mme. Brigitte told me I must never wear it with yellow."

"She did send a list of colors but I misplaced it somewhere. I so want to wear this bonnet."

"You can wear it with a green gown tomorrow. Don't you have other bonnets from the shop? I mean, do you have other bonnets?"

"I've two more."

The maid brought the bandboxes in a trice. Lady Maria selected the one trimmed with bombazine and velvet, all intricately pleated, with a plain brooch for adornment. Lady Barrington didn't look very enthusiastic but allowed Maria to place the bonnet on her head and tie the ribbons in an unconventional style.

'My. It sure looks nice!" her maid gasped.

Lady Maria led Amy to an armoire which had a mirror fixed to it. Amy was all smiles when she saw her reflection. "Let's go!" she said, linking arms with her new friend.

"I didn't know you were coming to Mayrick Manor. I had told Lord Daventon I wanted to meet you. He and my husband were together at Eton. When he first called, I felt I already knew him well. He is so kind and understanding. It has been terribly boring, not being able to move out. I enjoy his visits tremendously. He takes my side during my spats with Barrington! He is as good and kind as you are. You are both well matched. My felicitations."

Lady Barrington happily chattered on, mostly about Lord Daventon. "Though he doesn't show it, the scandal about his mother wounded him badly. But he is a noble son. He spends all his time with her, trying to get her well enough so that she can travel. He wants to heal the breach and take her home with him."

'So that is why the earl had not called on her. What was behind the engagement? Was that also for his mother's benefit? Even if it was, it did him credit,' thought Lady Maria.

They stayed out in the garden for as long as Lady Barrington desired. After a short walk, they had found a charming rustic seat with a view of the parterre gardens. It was a peaceful scene which Lady Barrington's inconsequential chatter did nothing to disturb.

"What's wrong? Are you unwell?" Lady Maria asked when Amy grew silent.

"I was thinking about scones. Shall we go in? I seem to be hungry all the time!"

They met Lord Barrington coming from the stables. He had ridden over to Wrenrose to see Daventon. He made a leg to Lady Maria and said he was pleased to see her. Drawing Amy to his side and tucking her hand in his arm, he complimented her on her glowing looks.

"That's because of Lady Maria! She helped me with the bonnet, and did something with the ribbons."

Her husband wrapped his arm around her waist. "Silly chit. It's not the bonnet. It's you. The country air suits you."

Lady Barrington looked at Maria and gurgled, her eyes dancing. "This is better than the geese and the ducks!"

Dinner at the Mayrick house party was the only time of the day when all the guests came together. The other meals were cold buffets, or trays sent up. Lady Severn came down in time for dinner. She had napped for some time and said she felt refreshed. But Lady Maria thought she looked frail and worn out.

Lady Barrington came in on her husband's arm. She wore a green brocade gown with beading and it became her very well. Lady Maria chose a simple gown of pink satin trimmed with white, and a long sash. Her hair was swept to a side and arranged in loose curls which were kept in place with a silver clip inlaid with pink pearls, to match the gown. A strand of pearls completed the picture of understated elegance.

It was an enjoyable meal. Lord Barrington was seated beside her and Lady Barrington was across them, wedged between Lady Havisham and Lord Turner, both evincing greater pleasure in each course that was served than in speech.

Lady Barrington tried to carry on a conversation with Lady Maria across the expanse of the table. She was like a naughty schoolgirl, holding up her napkin to make a funny face. Lady Maria was hard put to maintain her composure, especially as Barrington beside her snorted with suppressed laughter. She couldn't remember when she had such a good time. There was much to be said about a gathering in which matchmaking and flirtation did not occur. Then again, she would have enjoyed any of the *ton* events if she had Amy's unaffected friendship.

After dinner, some of the guests settled to whist in the library and others drifted into the drawing room. Lady Barrington picked up the harp and coaxed a pretty tune out of it. She was quite accomplished. Lord Barrington lounged beside Lady Maria. "I wish Daventon would join us. Does he know you are a guest here?"

Lady Maria shook her head.

"I thought not. I'll send a footman with a note tomorrow morning."

Lady Maria didn't know what to say. She started playing with the fringe of her sash.

Barrington sensed her unease. "I'm an addlepated twit, always blundering into what is not my business. Daventon knows when he should come visiting."

***

That night, once again sleep eluded Lady Maria. Amy had painted a picture of a good and decent man. Barrington had high praise for him and his accomplishments. Since her comeout, she had not met anyone with even a third of the earl's qualities. By jilting him she would hold him up to the *ton*'s ridicule. Would it be wiser to marry him instead? Her resentment against the nobility, which was rooted in her anger against the duchess, was ebbing. An earl who was a decent man would prove to be a suitable husband. One so understanding of his mother's predicament would help her buy back her parents' plantation.

Yes. She would do that. Evenson was someone she had met by chance. She couldn't wait for him. He had not made any move. What did she have to go upon, except a shared look of love and longing? Yet, for all of Amy's praise, she could not help but think Lord Daventon a cold man. He was prepared to enter into matrimony without so much as meeting her.

What was she to do?

***

Not too many miles away, the object of Lady Maria's thoughts was also awake. Sunk in a leather armchair, his feet propped up on the table, he sat nursing a glass of brandy. His mother's words played in his mind. She was emphatic about him marrying for love. When Barrington spoke of Amy, though it might be to complain about how pettish she had become, his face was suffused with a glow and a smile lit up his eyes.

Daventon had never experienced the emotion until a beautiful young woman had twirled in the center of a dusty London lane, raising her face to be kissed by warm sunshine. He knew what he felt for her was love. As unlikely as it was, he had fallen in love with her. But what he had told his mother still held. Family and Laura's happiness came first. While his views about love and marriage were shifting, his resolve to keep scandal at bay was firm.

He had to stop thinking about Milady. He would visit Mayrick Manor tomorrow. A day spent with Amy and James would help take his mind off his thoughts.

*** 

The fine weather held. Lady Maria was an early riser and especially when she was in the country, hated staying late in bed. Without calling for Gwen who slept in the adjoining dressing room, she changed into a simple calico gown.

The servants were up and silently going about their tasks. "My lady, breakfast is served," a footman said, leading her into the morning room. It faced east and the French windows were partly open to let in the fragrant breeze. Eager to be out in the morning air, Lady Maria made a quick breakfast of chocolate and some buttered toast. "Which way is the folly?" she asked.

An hour later, with her sketchbook and pencils tucked in her pocket, Lady Maria went up the stone steps that led to the folly. She had left a message for the duchess and for Gwen. They knew her ways and wouldn't worry. Her new friend Amy wouldn't miss her either. She'd confessed she never woke up before noon.

The folly was small but picturesque. Made during the reign of Richard II, it was well kept. The ancestor who had the making of it must have done so after a Grand Tour because it was decidedly European.

Lady Maria found a spot that shielded her from the stiff breeze. Behind her was a grassy slope, with daffodils and daisies, and in front a carved façade with vines and cherubs. Surrounding the folly was an apple orchard.

Lady Maria removed her bonnet. She leaned back against the pillar and pulled up her knees to rest her sketchpad. It wasn't a ladylike pose but it was comfortable. For a few moments she soaked in the smell of dew and grass, and the clean country air. She had come up to sketch some new designs because that would keep her troubled thoughts at bay.

During the long sleepless hours she had arrived at a decision. She would wait until she met the earl before jilting him. If he was the person Amy described, and if Evenson did not approach her by that time, she would marry Lord Daventon. This she would do after he promised to take her to America, and to help her in buying back the plantation.

Lady Maria started with a bonnet for Amy, one that would reflect her personality of exuberance touched with a natural shyness of manner. But she could not put her mind to it. After three attempts, she let her thoughts drift. Her hand began to move on its own accord, and deft strokes gave shape to a handsome face. Taking a darker pencil, she shaded in the beautifully shaped mouth and the aristocratic nose. She did the eyes next, making them intense and direct.

"You are very good."

Lady Maria jumped up, scattering pencils and sketchpad. Her mouth fell open. Had she conjured him up? What was Evenson doing, miles away from London, on this secluded spot?

She blinked. He was real. She watched him raise a finger to move a bothersome tendril away from her face. Only, the finger remained on her cheek, the touch a soft caress. Her eyes fluttered shut and her lips parted. She swayed, or perhaps it was the earth that tilted. At least that is what it felt like as Evenson brought his arms around her and gathered her close to his heart.

How my heart beats! Lady Maria thought and realized she was listening to Gareth's heart as she was pressed against his chest. The knowledge made her smile and snuggle closer. She was oblivious to everything else except the musk and lemon fragrance that surrounded her and the strength of his hold.

Daventon's gaze lingered on the disarray of auburn curls spilling onto his sleeve and the curve of the soft cheek pressed against the button of his greatcoat. Tenderness swept all rational thought. He held her a little away and raised her face to his. The same longing that surged through him filled her eyes. Wordlessly, as if in a dream, her arms slid around his neck. She arched closer within the circle of his arms and their lips met in a kiss that was searing in its gentleness.

"Milady!" Daventon murmured and let her step back. She raised a hand to her tremulous lips.

"I never expected to find you here. I saw the folly and decided to climb the hillock. My horse is tethered below. I didn't see you until I was standing behind you. As I said before, you draw very well."

Lady Maria blushed and grew confused. What explanation could she give for the sketch? She turned away from him and sat down by the pillar. Daventon lowered himself beside her.

Taking her hand in his, he said, "I've been thinking of you continuously. If I had your skill, I would have made dozens of portraits by now. But my drawing would have made you look like a character out of a Punch and Judy show."

Lady Maria knew he meant to ease the moment and loved him all the more for it.

Picking up her sketchpad he asked, "May I keep the drawing?"

Lady Maria nodded. She liked the thought of him having something made by her.

"On second thoughts, you keep it. Do you have a self-portrait?"

He flipped through the pages until he found one. He held it out to her. "May I keep this?"

Lady Maria nodded again and watched as he carefully tore out the page and buttoned it inside his coat, next to his heart.

"Milady, what are you doing here? Do you belong to these parts? Do you have family here?"

Lady Maria didn't know what to say. Gareth thought she was a shop girl. Disclosing her identity could put a distance between them. It could also show her in a rather sordid light. She would have to wait until he knew her better.

"I'm here with the Duchess of Severn."

The duchess! Lady Maria, his affianced bride! How had he forgotten about them! He was not free to receive kisses or bestow them.

He rose to his feet. "Milady, I hope you will forgive my behavior. I had no right …to do what I did. Please forget what happened. It shouldn't have and it's all my fault. I should have known better. I crave your pardon."

Momentarily stunned, Lady Maria found the use of her tongue. "No. Wait. You just said that you…have been thinking about me."

Daventon looked away. Maria also stood up. A horrible thought came to her. "Is it because…you think less of me because I let you…"

"No. I couldn't think more of you if you were a real lady born and bred. My circumstances stand in the way of our coming together. Nothing will come of this except a dalliance and I will not subject you to that."

Lady Maria stamped her foot as angry tears threatened. "Well, you should have remembered your circumstances before…before mauling me!"

Daventon tried to take her arm but she vehemently pushed him away. "Don't you dare touch me!"

"I'm sorry."

"Again? I don't want your apology. I want to understand what's keeping us apart."

"I'm sor… all right, I'm not. Dash it! I'm sorry I lost my head. The first time I saw you in the street, I lost my head. I knew you were the woman for me just as I knew I couldn't have you. I found reasons to go by your shop. It was a good thing I had pressing family matters that took me out of London. Otherwise, I would have made a fool of myself long ago."

"The reason, Gareth."

"You must not think it is your station. I would not mind for myself but there are those whose needs come before my own. In a way, I'm glad I met you here and we are having this conversation. Milady, there is no hope for us. We must stop thinking about each other and dreaming of a life that can never be."

"Do you...love...me?" Lady Maria asked, ready to confess who she was.

"I don't believe that love forms the basis of a good marriage. In fact, it complicates matters."

"You speak like the *ton*. Is that what you aspire for, a marriage of convenience?"

"They are the best sort," Daventon said and walked away.

"Give me back my sketch! I hate you!" Lady Maria called after him, and when he disappeared from sight, burst into tears.

Daventon sprang up on his horse and put it to gallop. He didn't want Barrington to see him. He had come early because Barrington had told him they would ride together whenever he called.

It would be wise to leave Wrenrose. If Barrington told Lady Severn that he was in the vicinity, it wouldn't do at all. But his presence was having a salubrious effect on his mother's health. He couldn't move her in her present condition.

Finally, he decided on sending a note and hoping for the best.

When Lord Barrington came down for a late breakfast, he received a missive from his friend that caused him some surprise. It read:

*My dear Barrington,*

*I regret that due to extenuating circumstances, I will not be able to join the party. I trust you will understand and not mention my presence at Wrenrose to her grace and Lady Maria, who I understand are at Mayrick Manor.*

*I remain...*

***

Lady Maria dried her tears. She would have to go back to the house if she didn't want a search party sent after her. Better to go before the whole house was astir.

Gwen was down in the kitchen, having breakfast. Lady Maria was not given to headaches but felt the beginning of one. It would be nice to slip back into bed. It would also invite attention. When Gwen returned, she found Lady Maria busy with her sketchbook. Knowing that she liked to work in silence, Gwen went on with her tasks, stopping only to inquire which gown she wanted her to lay out.

Lady Maria shrugged and went on with her sketching.

"It's a fine day. Shall I take out the sprigged muslin that came in last week?"

Her mistress continued to ply her pencil.

"The floral pink with the empire waistline? That becomes you well."

"I'll wear whatever you lay out for me, Gwen."

Gwen gave her a surprised look and then put down her disinterest to the slovenly nature of the party.

When Lady Maria came down, Lady Barrington was all set to take a turn in the rose garden. She had taken her friend's advice and teamed the bonnet with a green gown which was cunningly trimmed with white petit point lace.

"How do I look? Is the bonnet at the right angle? I never realized that made such a difference until yesterday."

Lady Maria tipped it forward by an inch, letting the sprig of delicate blossoms fall forward. Amy gave a contented sigh. Her cup of happiness was full.

"Shall we go outside? Oh, I'm sorry. Have you broken your fast?" she asked.

Lady Maria assured her she had been down earlier, and eaten.

"What did you do all morning?" Lady Barrington inquired, linking her arm with Maria's.

"I … I went for a walk."

Lady Barrington glanced at her. "You don't look like you enjoyed it much. Did you go alone? It's never fun to do things alone. *I know.* I've not had anyone to talk to, except for Barrington, and he doesn't have much patience to listen to fashion talk. Lord Daventon is better. The first time James brought him home, I was so bored I was in tears. His lordship pulled me out of the mopes soon enough. He said I must call him by his given name. I like him. I'm so happy you are marrying him because that means we'll see a lot of each other."

Lady Maria gave her an answering smile and complimented her on her gown. The rest of the day passed easily.

It set a pattern for the days to follow. Lady Maria was seldom without Amy's company. Amy liked to talk about her home, her parents, fashion. Maria was struck by the difference in their lives. Amy was almost her age. But the gap in their outlooks was immense. Amy was like a protected child, secure in the love of parents, siblings, and husband.

"I'm Papa's best girl. He was always bringing me pretty things and leaving them about the house, to surprise me. What I miss most is his hug. My mother's too. We are very close. It seems disloyal to miss them because James loves me very much. So do his parents. The duke says I'm the daughter he never had."

Lady Maria smiled at Amy, encouraging her to tell her more. She found it diverting, and also painful. This pain had nothing to do with Gareth. It rose from the void left by her parents' death, and the vacuum of growing up without a single hug.

The duchess was happy that Lady Maria had found a friend in Amy. They were always together, often breaking the stillness of the party with laughter. Gradually, Lady Severn realized that all the laughter came from Amy. She was the one doing the talking. Maria was as charming as ever, the Sweet Maria much admired by the *ton* but when she sat by herself, her eyes held a sadness reminiscent of her childhood.

Gwen also noted her low spirits. "What happened? Is it Mr. Evenson?" she asked.

Tears welled up in Lady Maria's eyes.

"You love him very much, don't you?"

"I detest him. I want to forget him."

"You will forget him after you wed the earl. Everyone who knows him speaks highly of him."

"Gwen, I can't marry him."

"You are in love with Mr. Evenson. I thought he was partial to you. But dear, I don't know what to think. I was hoping he would call at the shop. He is a gentleman, that's for sure. If he knew you were a lady, he would have come."

*I found reasons to go by your shop. I would have made a fool of myself long ago.*

"Gwen, if he truly loved me, he wouldn't have cared about my station."

"You must not judge in haste, dear. Not everyone is free to follow their heart."

"You mean, not everyone is strong enough. My father gave up everything for my mother. But Gareth says his circumstances will not allow us to come together. What circumstances? My father threw away a dukedom!"

"Did you see Mr. Evenson? Does he know you are Lady Maria?"

"I didn't get the opportunity of telling him. He took me by surprise," Lady Maria said and told Gwen everything. Well, not everything but she would have been surprised to know how much her face gave away.

"What do you want to do?" Gwen asked.

"I can't marry Lord Daventon."

"You'd never intended to marry him, remember? You wanted to jilt him at the altar and sail to America."

Lady Maria sighed. Life had been easier when she had her anger to sustain her. Now she couldn't subject her grandmother to more scandal. And the earl didn't deserve to be made a public spectacle.

"I'll speak to her grace tomorrow and tell her I've changed my mind. I don't want to wed the earl or anybody else. I want to return home."

# Chapter 12

While Stubbs was not of an inquisitive disposition, he believed in the power of information. For this purpose, he had developed a network of sharp-eyed urchins. Whenever he wanted to find out something, the word was out and the young imps kept a lookout for him.

After the incident with Lady Maria which had ended with him taking a leap out of his office window, he had set about finding out more about her and her mysterious rescuer. Unknown to them, he had slipped into an alley that led to a dingy shop right in front of his office. From behind its grimy windows he had observed them.

"Young love," his friend had murmured.

"A mystery is what I see. That woman is dressed like an upper servant but she's of the gentry. Does the man know her identity? He's definitely a nob."

"Want me to send out the word to tail them?"

At that very moment, Lady Maria stepped into her carriage and it started. Daventon stood looking after it, and this gave Stubbs sufficient time to send Jenkins, a most resourceful lad, to follow him. He was back within the hour. "'E's the Earl of Daventon," he said, thrusting a grimy hand for the promised two pence.

Stubbs kept abreast of society news. He knew of Lord Daventon's betrothal to Lady Maria. If his lordship was meeting a beautiful young woman who was in disguise, the situation was one of intrigue. He could use it to his advantage: a little blackmail went a long way in loosening purse strings.

Before he could delve deeper into the matter, Jenkins brought him inconvenient information. A runner had been heard making inquiries about a man who went by the names of Willie or Simpson, or Stubbs. He had a hand drawn picture with him, and was going from shop to shop.

Stubbs gave a resigned shrug. He would have to disappear into one of his numerous hideouts. The time wouldn't be ill spent, though. He needed a new alias and a disguise. Perhaps this time he would become a clergyman. People, especially women, trusted clergymen and confided in them.

Five days later, when Stubbs emerged from hiding, it was to a most puzzling news.

At first, Jenkins wouldn't tell him all unless Stubbs gave him six pence for his troubles. The punch on his nose and the purple bruise around his eye were worth the amount, he said. A cuff on the ear set matters on course. The *mort* was of the nobs and her name was Lady Maria. Her grandpa had been the *dook* and she lived in the house that had the *purty* gardens everyone gawked at through the gate.

"Severn House?"

Jenkins gave a sullen nod but brightened considerably when Stubbs added another two pence to the promised one.

"Who told you?"

"Tom."

"Tom?"

"He's the one working in that fancy shop at the corner."

Stubbs knew which one Jenkins meant. It was the bonnet shop carriages flocked to.

Jenkins explained how he had found out Lady Maria's identity. He had teased Tom mercilessly about working in a 'sissy shop'. This had led to fist cuffs and a tumble. Stubbs should have seen the fight! His bruises were nothing! He had given Tom a thorough dusting.

Stubbs lightly cuffed him to bring him back on track and learned that Tom had proudly informed Jenkins that his position was one of immense trust. A lady owned the shop. She dressed like a commoner for a lark but owned carriages and grand clothes. The diamond on her ring was as bright as a star.

Stubbs dismissed Jenkins and paid a visit to the gateman of Daventon's club where he learned that Lord Daventon had gone to Wrenrose. A stable boy at Severn House provided the intelligence that Lady Maria was at Mayrick Manor. Mayrick Manor and Wrenrose were in the same county!

Stubbs called upon a friend who could be trusted to know the latest *on dit;* he was Lady Goodall's coachman and a man of exceptional hearing.

"My lady is sure the engagement is a sham. Lord Daventon hasn't been seen since it was announced.

Lady Maria doesn't mention him at all. My lady, bless her, knows *what* is *what*," he informed Stubbs.

Stubbs pondered over the bits of information. Blessed with an imagination that would do credit to the secret police of any nation, he concluded that the fancy duo had hatched a plan to steal the Indian antique recently arrived. The sham engagement, the lady's disguise, and the plan to sail to America could mean nothing else.

"What do you think, Oliver?" he asked his longtime confidant.

"Seems far-fetched."

"That's because you don't know about the antique. It was all in the papers. Lady Mayrick's son got it off a Rajah. Four armed guards brought it from India. It has gemstones bigger than the egg of a duck."

"Blimey! You don't say so!"

"I'd long thought to try lifting it but antiques leave a trail. They are too much trouble for the likes of me to sell. I bet the earl has buyers queued up in America. To avoid suspicion, the lady will sail with it using the false name of Gwen Mathews. It all ties up. I couldn't have thought of a better plan myself."

"Why would they steal?"

"I dunno. Must be gaming debts."

Oliver scratched his head and thought it over. He made a good living out of a pair of loaded dice and a pack of cards that always favored him but his faith in the English nobility was strong. Now, had Stubbs told him a French count was planning to steal, he would have accepted it as the gospel truth.

"Sounds like a lot of moonshine to me," he responded.

"Much you know about what goes on with the gentry. There have been gentlemen robbers, some of them really talented. But it mostly gets hushed up. Family name and all that."

"What do you plan to do?"

"The antique isn't in my line of work. I'll go down to the country and tell them I know what their game is. That'll make them cough up a little blunt."

\*\*\*

Stubbs stopped at the inn on the road to Wrenrose. Except for his white shirt, his clothing was all black. A wooden crucifix and a black tri-corn completed his outfit. After breaking fast on a choice pie and a tankard of robust ale, he sauntered over to the innkeeper, hoping to gain information about the earl. Unfortunately, the innkeeper was not representative of his class; he was taciturn and rather morose.

Stubbs paid his shot and went to the stables, where his 'borrowed' horse was munching on some straw. "Give him some oats, will you?" Stubbs told the stable boy, pressing tuppence into his hand.

After the boy brought the oats, he struck up a conversation with him. The boy told him that Lord Daventon rode up to the inn now and then. His mother had lived at Wrenrose for several years but this was his lordship's first visit.

'Ah! That's because he's after the antique. Lady Maria is a guest at Mayrick Manor. He's staying at Wrenrose so that no one will suspect them when she steals the antique and passes it on to him!' Stubbs thought, marveling at his own intelligence.

Just then his lordship rode up on a magnificent horse. The innkeeper, pulling at his forelock, came out from behind his counter and shouted for a clean glass for his lordship. Stubbs lingered in the courtyard until Daventon took a seat, and followed him in. He made a polite bow and slid into the chair opposite Daventon.

The innkeeper frowned at Stubbs and jerked his chin in the direction of a vacant table. Obviously, he wasn't a churchgoing man because he showed scant respect for the clergyman garb.

Stubbs ignored the innkeeper and gave his lordship a beatific smile. Daventon wanted to be left alone. In his present state of mind, anyone smiling would have jarred on him but the wide smile flashing a gold tooth he found particularly obnoxious.

Stubbs leaned forward. "I have heard a lot about the Indian Antique at Mayrick Manor. Have you seen it, my lord?"

Daventon gave him a blank look.

"You know the one I'm talking about, my lord. The one with a lion and an elephant fighting to death, all studded with heathen gems."

Any person familiar with the upper echelons of society would have slunk away at the disdain in my lord's eyes. Stubbs interpreted it differently. Dropping his voice to a conspiratorial whisper, he said, "My lord, treat me as a friend, nay, as your servant! I know you want the piece and that's nothing to be ashamed of. In my field, we respect free enterprise. A man's birth needn't stand in the way of his natural talent."

Once again, he flashed a smile.

Lord Daventon responded to the piece of vulgarity with a glacial stare. When Stubbs continued to smirk, he snapped, "Good sir, I haven't the slightest interest in any piece of antiquity, Indian or otherwise."

Stubbs smirked and wagged his eyebrows suggestively. Leaning closer, he said, "Your secret is safe with me, my lord."

"You are mistaken, sir. Or perhaps touched by the sun."

Stubbs looked at him pityingly. Then he looked at him knowingly. And then he wagged a finger in his face.

Daventon wasn't a violent man but there is only so much a man blighted in love can take. And if the man in that position is a peer of the realm, the portion of what he will take is considerably reduced. Without warning, he shot out his fist and planted Stubbs a facer. It knocked him out of his chair. It probably knocked out a tooth too. If there was justice to be had in the world, it ought to have been the golden one.

The innkeeper came forward. "Don't sully your hands with the likes of him, milord. Little Joe here will do it for you," he said, bunching a ham-like fist and glaring at Stubbs who was trying to get up.

"Easy, Little Joe. He's a man of the cloth."

"That's what I meant, milord. Leave the likes of him to Little Joe. They be the ones causing the most trouble," he said, proving what Stubbs had suspected: he was not a churchgoing man.

Lord Daventon helped Stubbs up and much to Little Joe's disappointment, let him leave the inn without further retribution. The altercation with Stubbs and its absurdity restored his good humor. He decided to ride over to the old ruins.

Blocks of stone, burnt brick, and crumbling mortar piled in heaps around a squat blackened structure greeted him. There wasn't anyone else about. Leaving his horse to graze, he walked around a bit. The day was serene and cloudless. He stretched out on the grass, put his hands under his head and shut his eyes.

And sighed.

It was only five days since he had seen Milady but it seemed like an eternity. In a bid to stop thinking about her, he tried to keep himself occupied. There was the work on Wrenrose. He had employed gardeners and skilled workers to restore it to its former beauty. He supervised them and also drew his mother into the discussions. She was already taking an active part, even writing to haberdashers for samples, and discussing modern stoves with the housekeeper.

And yet, a part of him was always with Milady. He kept her likeness in a ledger, the pages of which were all blank. Every morning he retired to the library, purportedly to attend to the post but spent most of the time looking at the sketch. He carried the ledger to his bedroom, and sometimes it accompanied him on his rides. If his mother noticed, she did not comment.

He took to riding out by himself every day, stopping at the local inn, and spending time at places where he could be alone with his thoughts.

He had been right about love; it caused a lot of trouble. How did one get rid of it? Did he even want to get rid of it? Life without Milady would be empty but a life without thinking of her would be desolate, bleak. Feeling the way he did, how could he marry Lady Maria? Was this how his mother had felt? He knew, from his father's ramblings, that she had loved another when he had married her. If he married Lady Maria, would history repeat? He knew now that love happened. If Lady Maria fell in love with him while he pined for Milady, she would suffer.

"I can't marry Milady, that'll cause a scandal," he told the horse contentedly nibbling grass close by. "The best thing will be to break my engagement. Now that Mother is better, she and Aunt Nell can help Laura find a good husband. I'll marry Milady after Laura is wed so that no scandal affects her chances. Plague take it! I can't break my engagement without that causing a scandal!"

# Chapter 13

Lady Maria slept fitfully but rose at her usual early hour. Choosing a soft blue gown with a pale rose trim, she let Gwen help her get ready. Neither spoke about what was uppermost in their thoughts: breaking the engagement.

As soon as Lady Maria exited her bedroom, a footman informed her that Lady Barrington was awaiting her in the breakfast room.

Wreathed in smiles, looking as happy as a well-cared for child, Amy welcomed her with an embrace. "I told my maid to wake me up early. I want to spend as much time in your company as I can. The party is breaking up. The Wilsons left this morning and James says we should leave after luncheon."

Lady Maria took Amy's hands in her own. "Thank you, Amy. Your friendship means a lot to me."

She meant it. Though she has several friends among the *ton*, they were no more than old acquaintances with whom she exchanged common place utterances. Amy had won her over with her artless chatter and open friendship. She would have liked to tell her all about

Evenson and the engagement she wanted to end. But her reserve was of long standing, building up since she had come as a child to a vast mansion filled with curious servants and a cold woman who wouldn't acknowledge her presence.

"You must come for the christening of my baby. Lord Daventon is to be the godfather. I want you to be godmother."

Lady Maria swallowed as her throat constricted with emotion but managed to say all that was proper.

Lord Barrington joined them for breakfast and commenced teasing his wife about some trifling matter. Lady Amy appealed to Maria for help. Between the two of them, they soon had my lord offering an abject apology. This set them off giggling like school girls. By the time the meal ended, they were hooting with laughter in a most unladylike manner.

"Amy, you are good company! I don't remember when I laughed this much!" Lady Maria said, dabbing away a tear.

"Lady Maria, you must visit us in London. Amy is sorely in need of congenial company. She is well and truly tired of mine," Lord Barrington said.

His lady gave him a saucy look. "In that case, you will not mind if I dismiss you now, my lord?"

"Minx."

Lady Barrington inclined her head and curtsied. "Maria, shall we walk to the folly? Lady Mayrick tells me it is of exceptional beauty."

Lady Maria was dismayed at the prospect of returning to the folly. Fortunately, Lord Barrington dissuaded his wife and suggested they walk somewhere close to the house. Amy agreed and they took a turn on the gravel path surrounding the parterre gardens. With her delicate hued gown and bonnet of bleached straw, Lady Maria looked a picture of serene beauty.

Lady Barrington sighed. "I'm afraid you will be too busy to visit me when we are in London. There is Lady Malloy's ball and so many other events."

"They are all in the evening. I'll see you during the day."

"You can come visiting with Lord Daventon! How did he propose? He wouldn't tell me when I asked and James dragged him away to the library."

"Um… well…"

"Shall I tell you how James proposed? It was at an assembly dance and my card was full. James would have none of it. He struck off the first name on the card and wrote his name. Mr. Lord, whose name he had struck off, objected. James told him we were affianced and Mr. Lord should excuse his impetuosity. But it was not true at all! He hadn't proposed to me. He said he couldn't bear …"

Thankful to have escaped so easily, Lady Maria kept the conversation on Lord Barrington's masterful courtship for as long as she could. Then she deftly moved on to the wedding gown and trousseau. All that time, her mind was on how Lady Severn would react to her decision. She was already planning the engagement ball and thinking of wedding dates.

"Amy, you mustn't overtire yourself. Shall we go in?" she asked as the day grew warmer.

"I confess I'm a little fatigued. I should lie down for a bit before the journey," Lady Amy said and they returned arm in arm to the house. Except for the servants, there wasn't anyone about. Some guests had left and the others were either in their rooms or in the library.

"I must see her grace," Lady Maria said, parting from Lady Barrington at the bottom of the majestic staircase.

***

"There you are, my dear!" Lady Severn exclaimed as Lady Maria crossed over to greet her. "I saw you in the garden with that sweet child. I hope you had a pleasant time. I hear she and Lord Barrington are leaving today. Shall we leave tomorrow?"

"As you wish, your grace," Lady Maria answered and decided she would speak to the duchess only after going back to London. There was nothing to be gained by upsetting her before the journey.

Lord and Lady Barrington left in the afternoon, with my lord chafing over the delay his lady caused by lingering over her farewells.

Without Amy's effervescent company, Lady Maria lapsed into unhappy reflections about the shallowness of the male species which lasted until Mr. Turner came into the drawing room. He remarked that Lady Maria looked bereft without the delightful Lady Amy. Ignoring Lady Maria's protests -which he couldn't hear - he sat down beside her and regaled her with anecdotes from his youth. Trapped between one end of the sofa and Mr. Turner's bulk, Lady Maria endured his monologue until she could leave without offending him.

She developed a headache which proved beneficial as it drove all thoughts of Gareth from her mind and helped her to sleep.

***

Daventon couldn't sleep at all. How was he to end his engagement and still remain a gentleman? He also had to meet Milady and tell her he was the earl who was engaged to her mistress but he loved her so would she please wait for him until he disengaged himself? And respectfully married off his sister? Milady seemed the passionate sort. If she was attached to her mistress, would she accept his suit? And why on earth did she want to buy that plantation in America?

# Chapter 14

Stubbs picked himself up and rode away from the inn. Unfazed by the cut on his upper lip which was no more than what he expected in his line of work, he contemplated his next move – a visit to Mayrick Manor. He had faith in Jenkins but it would be better to make sure that the young woman who had approached him was Lady Maria.

He stopped at a small farmhouse. His clerical garb and the fast-swelling lip, and above all his charming manner had the good wife bustling around him in a most satisfactory manner. She gave him a basin of cold water to bath the lip and a compress for the swelling. She invited him to do honor to her humble table. Stubbs graciously agreed and did justice to the bounty of the land laid before him. He could have lingered on for a day or two, or even three. But he was a professional man who took pride in his work. Until now he had never failed in any of his ventures and did not plan on starting now.

When he was ready to leave, the good wife lined up all her offspring, the last three sniveling and scowling, for his holy blessing. Rightly construing it as payment for her hospitality, he complied.

After having ridden sufficiently away from the farmhouse, Stubbs exchanged his tri-corn for an inconspicuous hat, replaced his cravat with a knotted handkerchief and scuffed his shoes a bit. When he was just short of Mayrick Manor, he picked up a path that was most likely used by servants and tradesmen. An hour later he was concealed in a hedge, his horse safely out of sight.

His hiding spot afforded him with a panoramic view of the house. A plain carriage, piled high with luggage, came into view. Some time elapsed before two young women came out of the house and stood in the arched entrance. One of them wore a traveling dress. The other was the woman he had met in his office. Her disguise had been good, he had to admit. He watched as she stood waving to the occupants of the carriage. Then she went indoors.

Stubbs spent considerable time in the shrubbery but couldn't get an opportunity to speak to Lady Maria. It was his experience that women were more sensible to the consequences of blackmail. But Lady Maria did not appear again. When a farm dog started showing an unhealthy interest in his backside, he decided to leave, all the while lamenting country houses which afforded little scope for slipping in notes through urchins and serving maids.

He stopped at a wayside barn for the night. Supper was apples from the orchard at Mayrick Manor, bread, cheese, and the mince pie the good wife at the farmhouse had given him for his journey.

The chirping of birds woke him at an early hour. After cleaning his face and shoes with good honest spit, he composed a note:

*Lord Daventon,*

*The Secret about your Lady Love is safe – for the Present. I shall be at the Old Ruins at Eleven o'clock.*

*XXX.*

Daventon received the note as soon as he woke up.

"Who brought this?" he asked the footman.

"The under-gardener, my lord. Someone gave it to him and said it was urgent."

Secret about his Lady Love is safe – for the present? Someone was blackmailing him about Milady!

Daventon hurriedly got dressed and was at the ruins by ten o'clock itself. The only person about was someone who looked like a prosperous innkeeper. He rose from the pile of stones he was sitting upon and bowed. Then he gave a dazzling smile – dazzling because of his gold tooth.

"You! What's your game?"

"My lips are sealed, my lord."

"Why did you call me if your lips are sealed?"

"I meant about the secret, my lord. Lady Maria's secret is safe with me. I'm a gentleman with the highest regard for the delicate sex. I don't want a lady's name to be bandied about."

"Lady Maria? You said my lady lo…never mind." Daventon guessed the man had called him because of his engagement to Lady Maria.

"Will a guinea suffice to sustain your gentlemanly behavior?"

"Twenty guineas is more like it but I'll take ten, milord, it being the matter of a lady's good name."

"Twenty guineas! What could you know about Lady Maria that is so damaging?"

Stubbs gave him a sly look and wagged a finger. "You know very well, milord. She dresses like a shop girl and makes bonnets."

"What?!"

"You put on a good act, milord, I'll give you that. I saw you with her in Smiths Lane. She was there to buy property in America."

Daventon couldn't believe his ears. Milady was Lady Maria! He barely heard the rest. Thrusting a handful of guineas in Stubbs' eager hands, he sprang up on his horse and disappeared in a dust of cloud. By the time he rode up to Mayrick Manor, he'd dropped his hat somewhere and carried enough dust on his person and clothes to startle the ancient butler into blinking his eyes.

"Lord Daventon to see Lady Maria!" he said, throwing the reins to a footman.

Without a word, the butler showed him into the morning room. Five minutes later, Lady Mayrick entered. Daventon bowed over her hand and was discomfited by the dust that covered his hessians.

He met Lady Maverick's quizzical look with an abashed one. "I crave your pardon, Lady Maverick, for coming in this state. May I see Lady Maria?"

"We aren't that fussy in the country, Daventon. Please be seated. It's ages since I saw you. Are you come down to Wrenrose? How is your dear mother?

"She is improving, my lady. My father's death was a blow to her."

"That was to be expected. She loved him very much."

Daventon saw that she was sincere. First Lady Severn and now Lady Mayrick, both didn't credit the vicious tales that had circulated about his mother. He would take their help to ease her way back into Society. She had been a recluse for far too long.

He brought his attention back to Lady Mayrick. She was saying something about Lady Maria. "Her grace wanted to make an early start. They left soon after breaking fast."

Daventon was sorely disappointed. After taking leave of Lady Mayrick he was tempted to ride to London. But the physician was coming in the afternoon and he wanted to discuss his mother's health with him.

\*\*\*

Dr. Coolidge was happy with the progress Lady Daventon had made.

"Is she up to a carriage journey? I want to take her with me to Daventon Hall."

"I don't see why not. Her ladyship is showing active interest in her surroundings. Her appetite has improved and she is out of the dismals."

Dr. Coolidge went so far as to discontinue the day nurse and stopping all cordials except one. After he left, Lady Daventon asked, "I see a marked change in you this morning. Where did you go? What has happened to make you look so happy and carefree?"

"Lady Maria."

"Lady Maria? I thought you didn't care for her. I thought your heart was engaged elsewhere."

"It's a long story."

"Tell me."

"I don't know the half of it! But rest assured. You wanted me to marry for love and by a happy chance that is what I shall be doing."

"Gareth! My felicitations! Am I to understand that you and Lady Maria had a lover's spat and it is all resolved?"

Daventon recalled Milady at the folly. She had stamped her foot and shouted at him. "Yes Mother, we had a quarrel," he said and Lady Daventon had to be satisfied with that.

"Gareth, you must return to London immediately. I thought you didn't care for Lady Maria's company but you mustn't linger here any longer. She will want you to squire her to the balls."

"Mother, we should go to Daventon Hall. Laura will be eager to see you."

"Shall we all go to London instead? It is time Laura had a Season. I must also meet Lady Maria for she is to be my daughter soon."

Daventon knew the prospect of going into society terrified his mother and she wanted to make the effort for her children. He told her Lady Severn and Lady Mayrick had inquired about her and his Aunt Nell thought kindly about her.

"Flanders tried to make me go to London during the Season, or to Bath. She said those who knew me wouldn't cut me and the others did not matter. But I had not the heart for gaiety and stayed put at Wrenrose. Edward didn't leave Daventon Hall either and the rumors about us ran wild. No one knew the truth and that gave rise to sordid conjecture. A heated quarrel over a misunderstanding parted us for life. I was certain Edward would ask me to return and waited for him to come calling."

"Mother, I know he came at least once. I heard him tell Aunt Nell. You were at Harrogate and had been ill."

"Gareth, don't jest with me! I was at Harrogate for my health and Flanders told me she had written to Edward. I thought he would come but he did not."

Briefly, with his face flushing, Daventon told her what he had overheard as a boy. He couldn't tell her how it had affected him. Lady Daventon's face turned pale and she clasped the pendant she always wore. In a voice shaking with emotion, she cried, "Edward saw me kissing the picture in this pendant and left?"

She opened the pendant and held it out to Gareth with a trembling hand. It held a miniature of the late Earl of Daventon.

"I had the likeness made in Harrogate. The artist had connections with the *ton* and had met Edward many times. He painted it from memory."

Daventon didn't want to distress Lady Daventon further but he had to know. "What happened to us, Mother? What made you and my father suffer so much? Why did Laura grow up without knowing you? You can't imagine the gossip and the snide comments that followed me at Eton."

Lady Daventon leaned back with a weary sigh. "I had my comeout at the age of sixteen. Just out of the schoolroom, I was already turning heads. Edward was twenty-four, and an earl. He presented his suit to my father. My father was a rather impoverished baron. He was looking for someone who would make a settlement large enough to cover his debts and provide for me and my siblings. Edward was so besotted he would have settled twice the amount. I came to know about the betrothal only after the papers were signed.

"I was infatuated with our vicar's son, Theodore. My father knew this and whisked me back to the country, allowing only a five-minute meeting with Edward. I had always been rather shy. Left alone with Edward in the library, I did not raise my eyes to his face.

"My mother died a month later and the wedding was postponed. During the long engagement, Edward became an ogre in my mind. I blamed him for taking me away from my home and from Theodore. Ours was an innocent love. We stole glances at each other in the church. Theodore gave me a corsage. It was at a Christmas ball. We were a small group. The boys gave corsages to the girls they danced with first. Theodore danced with me. Everyone knew I was engaged. While the other girls were teased about their admirers, nobody minded me because they knew I was spoken for.

"Theodore came to see us a fortnight later. He was leaving home to study under a tutor. By then I had got over my infatuation. Perhaps it was his fresh crop of pimples or his new found love for writing poetry that had put me off. As a parting gift, he gave me a book of sonnets, all penned by him. They were in the romantic style, with talk about dying of a broken heart, and worshiping the fair maiden from afar. The gift was as much a desire to preen over his newfound talent as a romantic gesture. He tied the book of sonnets with a ribbon and used his tie pin to hold the bow in place.

"I told you he was no longer the shining knight of my dreams. But which girl will throw away a book full of sonnets penned in her name?

"Edward and I were married a few weeks later. I no longer thought him an ogre but I was in awe of him. He was so handsome, and I felt tongue-tied in his presence. We went to Rome and to Paris for our wedding trip. Very soon, I was in love with my husband. I thought myself the luckiest woman on earth. Our happiness only increased with your birth and Laura's.

"One afternoon, Edward came into my sitting room, to share some happy news about a friend. Just then the maid informed me that Laura was crying for me. I told him I would bring Laura and left. Edward decided to use the time in penning a congratulatory note to his friend. He opened my writing desk for stationary and spotted a small box. He had purchased it for me in Paris. It was of enameled silver and had a cunning lock.

"He opened it and found a dried corsage of flowers interspersed with satin roses, a slim volume of poems addressed to me in a masculine hand, and a tie pin with a single pearl on an engraved T."

Lady Daventon shut her eyes as the scene swam in front of her again. She had returned from the nursery, matching Laura's baby steps, to find Edward taut with anger, breathing hard. "Madam, may I know the identity of your admirer?" he had demanded.

The box was open on the table and the contents scattered. He had lifted the tie pin and turned it this way and that. "A worthless trinket. It does not belong to a nobleman. It seems you have bestowed your favors very much below you.

"I have never wronged you, my lord".

"Only trifled with my feelings, and my gift."

He'd flung the box against the fireplace. It was strong and did not break. When she'd rushed forward, he had snarled, "Don't defile it with your touch."

He'd hurled the box into the fire and swept its contents into the flames. Then he had stormed out of the room, and from her life.

"What did he say?"Daventon asked, sitting beside her on the settee, and taking her cold hands in his.

"He accused me of adultery and was gone the next day. After waiting for two weeks, I returned to my father's house, bringing with me what I held the most precious: you and Laura. The next day, Mr. Meyers arrived. He brought a letter from Edward. I have it still. I was to send the children to him and stay away. He would spare me the scandal of a divorce if I moved to Wrenrose. My brother tried to intervene, so did Flanders. He refused to see them."

"He was angry. He loved you."

"He was angry and I was proud. I thought he would come for me. How could he not when I was the mother of his children? Finally, I sent him a letter. I said I was prepared to come back for the sake of the children. I thought that would heal the breach. But he loved me. He would have taken me back had I said I wanted to return for his sake. That is the problem with love. It needs nurturing."

"When was this?"

"Soon after Helena made her home with you. Edward wrote that his sister would care for the children and they would do better without my corrupting influence. He was there for the children and all his love was for them."

Daventon felt a pang at those familiar words. At times his father would smother them with love. They never knew what to expect. He would drink himself to oblivion and forget their presence or have bouts of remorse. Aunt Nell, bless her, shielded them from his moods.

"Aunt Nell was good to us. I don't know what we would have done without her. Especially Laura."

"She has been a good influence. I always thought you and Laura would grow up hating me."

Daventon looked away. Over the years his heart had hardened against his mother. He resented it that she was happy with someone while his father suffered. Yet he hadn't hated her; he'd turned bitter and tried to shut her out of his thoughts. When Mr. Meyers had told him about her failing health, he had come to make his peace with her. He hadn't expected her to be distraught over his father's death, or that his feelings would change at the sight of her.

Lady Daventon said, "I tried to hate your father but love cannot be uprooted at will. When he died, I lost the will to live."

They sat in silence for several minutes until Lady Daventon said she would go to her room and lie down until supper.

Daventon would have none of it. "Let's sit in the garden. The sunshine will serve you better than Dr. Coolidge's cordial," he coaxed and gave her his arm. They walked to the topiary and to the duck pond. Daventon recalled incidents from his childhood, especially the time he had spent with her, and made her smile. All through supper, he showered her with loving attention.

When Lady Daventon went to bed, it was with a resolve that she would shake off the past and make a new life with her children.

# Chapter 15

The next morning, Daventon found his mother firm on the London scheme. "Gareth, I shall write to Lady Helena to bring Laura to Wrenrose. We shall spend a week or so here to prepare for the Season. We will all need a new wardrobe. You too, dear. You will cut a dashing figure if you would put your mind to it. You have the look of your father. Edward was considered quite the catch."

"Do we have the time to outfit Laura? James told me Lady Amy went to a lot of trouble to prepare for the Season."

"We will make do. Betty, our housekeeper's daughter, used to work for a well-known modiste in London until last year when she decided to marry a farmer and settle down in the village. She can make some of our gowns and the rest can be had in London. I'll send for her immediately."

Betty was excited about the proposal. She missed her earlier occupation and assured Lady Daventon she was competent to turn them out as well as any upscale modiste. "I've kept up with the latest fashions and know all the right shops. If you will open accounts with them, I can bring back samples. We have very little time. I will need to engage two or three girls from the village."

Lady Daventon gave a brisk nod. "My dear, you will need to make several trips to London. My coachman will take you. Daventon, you must write to Mr. Meyers about opening accounts in those shops. Betty, give his lordship the list."

Daventon patiently noted down the list of shops Betty needed to visit, and also the traders who would not mind bringing their wares to Wrenrose.

"My lady, will you switch to half-mourning?" Betty asked.

"Yes, she will," Daventon said firmly, ignoring his mother's protests.

He was pleased to see his mother actively taking part in the preparations. "I'm determined to let go of the past. It is enough that Edward wanted me back. We were both foolish in not revealing our need for the other. I was the more to blame; I should have tried harder for the sake of my children," she confided during the course of the busy day.

For a busy day it was! The rosewood chest was removed from the attic. Lady Daventon wanted Betty to see whether any of the gowns were in the current mode; she wanted Laura to wear at least one of them. Most of them had been made in Paris, with Edward poring along with her over the fashion plates. The jewels were removed from the safe, to check whether they were in need of cleaning or polish. Once again, most of them brought back memories which Lady Daventon shared with her son.

During supper she asked, "Gareth, when are you going to London? Now that matters are resolved between you and Lady Maria, you must return to be with her."

"I don't want to leave you alone, Mother. I'll wait until Aunt Nell and Laura are here to keep you company."

"I insist you leave tomorrow. I plan to busy myself with Betty. There is also the work with the gardens and the house. I want Wrenrose to look its best when Laura arrives."

"I fear you will overtire yourself, ma'am."

"Better that than go into a decline!" answered Lady Daventon with spirit and was rewarded with a hug from her son.

"I'll leave tomorrow morning. I must also hire a house for the Season."

"There's no need for that," Lady Daventon said with a guilty look. "We only need to hire more staff for our townhouse."

Daventon mentally went over the list of properties he had inherited, and a townhouse in London did not figure in them. He raised a quizzical brow.

"When we parted ways, Edward sold the Daventon townhouse. It came up for sale again four years ago. Meyers asked Edward whether he should buy it back. When Edward refused, he mentioned it to me. I had barely been using the allowance your father made me and a considerable sum had piled up. I decided to buy it but could not do so in my name."

Daventon nodded; the law did not permit a married woman to own property.

"I'm afraid Meyers took Edward's signatures by deceit. He didn't want to but I insisted. The house held some good memories and it had been in the Daventon family for four generations."

"How about the upkeep of the house? I haven't seen any bills."

"Meyers created an annuity from my funds."

"Where is this house?"

"It's on the same lane as Severn House."

Same lane as Severn House! He would be living close to Lady Maria!

***

Lord Daventon arrived in London by midmorning. Before heading for Meyers, Meyers & Meyers, he stopped at his club where he had retained a room. He changed into a fresh shirt and a coat of fashionable cut that displayed well his neckcloth and complimented his fawn pantaloons. Instead of hessians, he chose a highly polished pair of tall boots.

Nat Stevenson brightened up at the sight of his lordship. Except for a lack of seals and fobs, and jeweled buckles on those boots, his lordship was dressed to a nicety. He came out from behind his desk to escort him in. But Lord Daventon went past him to the window and stood looking out into the street! Nat had to clear his throat several times before he could get his attention and show him into the office.

Mr. Meyers was eager to know how things were at Wrenrose. When Daventon mentioned the purchase of the townhouse, he looked abashed. Daventon put him at ease. "You did well, sir, to consider her ladyship's

161

wishes. We have much to do before my mother and sister come up to London."

Mr. Meyers rang for Nat. "Take down notes," he instructed.

Nat diligently listed the shops for setting up an account, the work to be carried out at Daventon House, and the staff to be hired.

"Mr. Meyers, I shall be needing a valet. My father's valet did well enough for me in the country but he is old now, and suffers from gout."

The notepad slipped from Nat's hand and he almost fell at his lordship's feet. "My lord, please engage me. You won't regret it at all. I know all there is to know about gentlemen's clothing. I can make The Oriental, The Mathematical, and The Osbaldeston. If you have a fancy for it, I can also tie a Mailcoach for which I recommend a kashmeer shawl rather than a cotton neckcloth!"

"That's enough, Nat," Mr. Meyers said.

Nat stood up and he had tears in his eyes. "Mr. Meyers, I mean no disrespect. I have always wanted to become a gentleman's gentleman."

"Nat, I don't doubt you will make a good valet but I can't deprive Mr. Meyers of your services."

"You will be doing me a favor," Mr. Meyers said dryly. "Nat has no interest in the clerkship and his work reflects it. I engaged him because his father worked in this position and wanted me to give his son a chance. I'll ask him to take Nat's place until we find someone else. Nat, you know your father will be disappointed, don't you?"

Nat nodded but looked blissfully happy and Mr. Meyers left it at that. It was decided Nat was to start valeting from the very next day.

When Lord Daventon came out of the office, he saw a familiar dark carriage coming down the lane. He slipped behind a wide tree and waited. The carriage came to a stop and the occupants alighted; Gwen first and Lady Maria after her. While Gwen unlocked the door, Lady Maria looked up wistfully at the window of Mr. Meyer's office.

Daventon stood gazing at her. She was pale and there were shadows under her eyes. Wasn't she sleeping well? How did she manage to look so different each time? The saucy young woman with that sweeping bonnet...bonnet? Was it a trick of the bonnet? The frilly cap she wore proclaimed her a shop girl.

But why did she go to the trouble of disguising her appearance? Why did she want to go to America? And the biggest question of all: why had she consented to an engagement with Lord Daventon, that too without meeting him?

His dear love was an enigma and he would know more about her before he revealed his identity. With a plan forming to that end, he sought out Lord Barrington and found him at White's, languidly perusing a newspaper sheet.

"Gareth! When did you come to London?"

"This morning. James, I need your help. My bailiff sends a lot of mail. I'll have it arranged to be delivered to you. My valet will pick it up from you every day."

"Mail going missing at the club? I've been telling you to move in with us."

"I'm moving out of the club today. I've engaged a valet. He'll take lodgings for me in the city under the name of Gareth Evenson. That's why I'm having my mail sent to you."

"What? Why? Are you a spy or something? Is it a matter pertaining to the Crown?"

"It pertains to matters of the heart. You were always telling me I was remiss in that direction."

Lord Barrington didn't look pleased. "Gareth, Amy and I spent some time with Lady Maria and I must say she is as good and noble as she is beautiful. No wonder everyone calls her Sweet Maria. She was kind to Amy, letting her chatter on and making her feel at ease. A genuine friendship has sprung up between them. If you mean to trifle with Lady Maria's feelings, I won't help you."

"Sweet Maria is quite the Paragon," Daventon said, putting on a sardonic air.

It did not go down well with Lord Barrington. "She could have her pick these last four seasons but she chose to honor the match arranged by her grace. You don't come up for the Season but you must know how popular she is. Last week she had a group of French noblemen trying to joust out her English suitors."

"What magic does she hold? Where does her allure lie?"

"I'll repeat what I heard one of her suitors say. She is beautiful but just short of perfection. She is vivacious but never loud. She is sometimes artless but never silly. And she never flirts. No dropping of gloves and handkerchiefs or throwing hints to garner compliments. She doesn't play with the sentiments of her suitors. Even in her refusal of their suit, there is kindness."

"Did Hennicker offer for her?" Daventon asked, recollecting the scene at the club.

"He did, though why he bothered beats me. She's turned down suitors by far worthier than him. Gareth, you're my friend but I can't help you. Lady Maria is worthy of my regard as well."

"Your scruples do you credit. Whatever I'm doing is to gain Lady Maria's trust. Our engagement was the result of an arranged match. I never expected to fall in love, and never wanted to fall in love, deeming it a quagmire. But we fell in love under peculiar circumstances and different identities. More than this I cannot reveal."

For once Lord Barrington was bereft of words. But not for long. "Different identities? Lady Maria met you as Gareth Evenson and didn't recognize you because you never come to London during the Season. While she is engaged to Lord Daventon, she is in love with Gareth Evenson!"

"I must say you have far more brains than I credited you with. They weren't in evidence at Eton, though, so you must not blame me for misjudging your capabilities."

"That's why Lady Maria didn't look happy when I told her I would write to you. She didn't want you at the Mayrick party. Wait till I tell Amy! This is the out and out of everything. Am I allowed to tell Amy?"

"Only if you are prepared for the consequences. She won't give you rest until she knows the whole of it. She may also tell Lady Maria and I don't want that."

"She'll ring a fine peal over my head when she knows!"

"I'll take the blame. Don't tell Amy I'm in London either. She will want me to come visiting and I might run into Lady Maria."

# Chapter 16

Lady Maria was no closer to breaking her engagement.

Three days ago they had left Mayrick Manor. Perhaps it was the morning air, or perhaps it was the pollen in the countryside. Whatever the reason, her grace developed a cold by the time they reached Severn House. This led her to banish Lady Maria from her presence.

Gwen was worried. Lady Maria was listless and had no appetite. She was always lost in her thoughts. The pile of invitations awaiting them on their return had gone unacknowledged. The morning callers were not being admitted with the butler informing them that the duchess and Lady Maria were rather indisposed. The only place she punctiliously visited was the bonnet shop. Gwen knew it was because she hoped to see Mr. Evenson there.

During their absence, Mme. Brigitte had been overwhelmed by orders and the highhandedness of her patrons. She had told the ladies she would not take orders for creating new designs and they would have to pick from the designs in her sketchbooks. If they wanted, she would select the ones that suited them best. This did not go down well, especially as it came from someone as mild mannered as Mme. Brigitte. If she was one for high drama or throwing a fit over something trivial, she would have earned their respect. Now they refused to listen. They must have new designs and she must make them! A duchess in her own right added an ultimatum. If Mme. Brigitte was not sensible to the honor they did by patronizing her shop, the duchess would have the shop removed. Poor Brigitte had buckled under the pressure and accepted all the orders.

Gwen was aghast when Mme. Brigitte handed her the bundle of papers. What was worse, orders for new bonnets kept pouring in and Lady Maria had no interest in designing them. In three days she had sketched only three bonnets, all of them merely passable. Her eyes kept straying from her sketchbook to the open window.

"Gwen, let's go home!" she said, pushing aside the papers irritably.

Gwen gathered up their things and sent word for the carriage. It was a silent ride as Gwen had run out of all topics they could converse upon.

Rosie was waiting for them eagerly. "My lady! Isn't it wonderful" she exclaimed. "Lord Daventon is moving into the house down the street!"

"What?"

Rosie, with help from the footman and the butler, enlightened Lady Maria that the vacant house on the street had been bought by the Earl of Daventon. He was bringing his mother and sister for the Season. A butler and a housekeeper had been engaged that very morning and now the house was a veritable hive of activity with workers giving it a proper cleaning.

"There's a man painting the Daventon family coat of arms at the entrance. Her grace will be pleased. She could never abide the coal merchant," the butler added.

"My lady, they are hiring more servants. Will you please put in a word for my sister? She's not happy in her present situation," petitioned Rosie.

Flustered, Lady Maria replied, "I don't know, Rosie. That depends on when I meet his lordship."

"Now you will be meeting him all the time, my lady," answered Rosie, which was exactly what Lady Maria feared.

Lady Maria managed to evade further questions and escaped into her room. "What should I do, Gwen?" she asked.

"If Lord Daventon calls, you must see him. Are you still decided upon breaking the engagement?"

"I have no doubt he is good and amiable. Amy likes him and she is not one to dissemble. But Gwen, you have told me about my parents and how much in love they were. It seemed like a fairytale to me. The *ton* marriages I saw had husbands and wives pursuant upon their own pleasure. Most wives were happy as long as their husbands gave them pin money and stayed away from them. After meeting Gareth Evenson, I know I can have the life my parents had. Anything less seems to me a sacrilege. That is why I must end this engagement; it is nothing more than a farce. And I must do it before Lord Daventon calls on us. Her grace is much improved, I'll speak to her after supper."

But that was not to be. The duchess received news about the demise of an old friend. It upset her to the extent that she stayed in her room. Lady Maria did not have the heart to add to her unhappiness. She would have to wait for a day and hope Lord Daventon didn't call on her before she had speech with her grace.

Lady Barrington sent a note in the evening. She knew dear Maria must be busy will callers during the mornings and with social events in the evenings which was why she was inviting her to break her fast with her. They would enjoy each other's company without discomfiting Lady Maria's social calendar.

Lady Maria accepted the invitation. Amy's lively chatter would do her good.

"You look well," Lady Maria said, greeting Amy with affection.

"Do I? It is this outfit though how long I will manage to fit in it, I know not! I shall look hideous, I expect, as my time gets near."

"You will only grow more beautiful," Lady Maria assured her, nibbling on a delicious croissant. They lingered over the meal, with Lord Barrington making an appearance only to be told pettishly by his wife that he must leave them alone because they had much to talk about.

And they did. They had a long, comfortable conversation about nothing in particular until Lady Maria said, "Amy, I must leave now but I'll come whenever I can, if it's all right with you."

Lady Barrington assured her she was always welcome. Her dear Maria need not stand on formality and she would look forward to her visits.

Just then Lady Edwina came calling. She was most effusive. "My dear Lady Maria, I can't thank you enough! Mme. Brigitte is divine! I now have bonnets to match all my morning dresses and none are alike!"

As she prattled on, Lady Maria had an idea about the bonnet shop. The new orders had become a pressing problem. She was not at all inclined to create those designs. The only face she saw was a clean-cut masculine one with a cleft in the chin and riveting blue eyes, and it was not at all conducive to planning bonnets and caps! She couldn't shut down the shop – Mme. Brigitte and her assistants would lose their livelihood. She needed a way for the patrons to order from the existing designs and not demand new ones.

She said, "Lady Edwina, I regret having revealed Mme. Brigitte's identity. Now she wants to shut the shop."

"What!" shrieked Lady Edwina.

"What!" quavered Lady Barrington.

"She is receiving far too many orders and has no time for designing. I know Mme. Brigitte well. She's a gentle creature and easily upset. I believe she is being harried by some customers who will not take no for an answer. Now she wants to close the shop."

"What about the orders she has taken? I've asked her to design a bonnet for a garden party!"

"Has she taken any advance? She told me she hasn't."

"She hasn't but..."

"Not to have any of those darling bonnets? Maria, you must do something!" Amy entreated.

"Amy, I spoke to her. I even withdrew my order and told her I would choose a bonnet from her pattern book. She has three books filled with designs. I thought she may reconsider if she needn't design anything new for the time being."

"I'll do the same! It will be horrid not to have any bonnet from her. I'll take back my order as well. And I'll tell everybody. Lady Maria, you can tell Mme. Brigitte she needn't worry. All those orders will be canceled. I'll see to that!"

Satisfied, Lady Maria took her leave.

"Do you think it will work?" Gwen asked when they were in the carriage, on their way to the bonnet shop.

"I hope so. If it doesn't, we'll just have to close the shop," Lady Maria answered.

Gwen extracted a drab pelisse from a bag. She helped Lady Maria into it. Next the satin slippers were exchanged for scuffed shoes, and the bonnet festooned with ribbon and netting was exchanged for the cap with the fringe of false hair.

When they reached the bonnet shop, it was to find two carriages waiting outside it, one of them belonging to Lady Goodall.

"Lady Maria, you mustn't leave the carriage. Lady Goodall is unrelenting in her pursuit of scandal. She mustn't see you. I'll have a word with Brigitte and we shall leave."

Gwen took the precaution of wrapping a scarf around her head. When she opened the door to the shop, she found a sealed letter on the floor. It was addressed to Milady Adam from Gareth Evenson. She locked the door and came back without speaking to Mme. Brigitte.

"Why are you back so soon? Did Lady Goodall see you?" Lady Maria asked.

In answer, Gwen gave her the letter and rapped on the roof of the carriage. The carriage started moving.

"Gwen, he wants to meet me! I'm to go to Kensington Gardens. He says he will wait there every evening! What am I to do?"

"You can't go, my dear. You will be ruined if anyone sees you."

"Gwen, I must see him and know what is behind his strange behavior at the folly."

"If you are recognized, the Severn name and the clout her grace enjoys will not save you. An assignation of this nature will give a bad name to a woman even in America."

"I'll be careful. You can't know how much this means to me!"

"I know but meeting in a public place can prove to be disastrous. Why don't you wait until he comes to Mr. Meyers' office? We'll arrange something then."

Lady Maria would not listen. She begged until Gwen relented. "You must promise you will meet him only this one time. You mustn't allow him to lead you into any deserted part of the garden. I'll come with you and stay close."

Lady Maria agreed to everything and rewarded Gwen with a fierce hug and a resounding kiss. Then she moved on to the next problem which was a big one: what was she to wear?

"I want to wear my new walking dress which is just come. But he thinks me to be in employment of the duchess of Severn. The dress is too fine for a ladies' maid."

"Are you not planning upon telling him the truth?"

"I want to wait until I know him better."

"You promised this would be the last meeting!"

"I won't meet him but...I don't know! What will he think if I tell him I'm a lady born and bred? Will he not think less of me for going about in disguise?"

Torn between trying to look her best and not revealing her identity, Lady Maria quickly decided upon the former. The walking dress was a modish creation of violet sarsenet and matched her eyes. Its sleeves were long and full, and it came with a pelisse of three- fourth length. The bonnet was of her own design, with clusters of violets on the brim and a short, stiff veil.

***

Adam brought around the carriage. Gwen had told him they were taking a turn as Lady Maria was in low spirits. As soon as they entered the garden Lady Maria asked, "Do you see him?"

Gwen didn't answer because she was busy looking around to see if any member of the *ton* was strolling about.

"Gwen! He's coming!" Lady Maria hissed, clutching Gwen's arm.

Daventon bowed to both of them and smiled at Lady Maria. Gwen tried to catch her eye but Lady Maria skipped ahead most inelegantly and took his proffered arm. Very soon it became apparent she had either forgotten or had no intention of following Gwen's advice.

Daventon strode towards a narrow winding path with Lady Maria tripping beside him. Though Gwen tried to keep up, the gap between them widened and they disappeared around a bend.

Gwen found them soon enough behind a tall topiary but didn't intrude. They looked blissfully happy as they held hands and gazed into each other's eyes. She walked back to the lane; to give them some time alone, and to stand guard so that they were not discovered.

"Mr. Evenson!"

"Gareth. Call me Gareth. My La..Milady."

"Why did you call me here?"

"To declare my love for you. And to get to know you."

Lady Maria didn't know what to say. Her eyes faltered from his intense gaze.

"You needn't tell me anything you don't want to. But I hope you will trust me with your secrets."

"Secrets?"

"You are a woman of mystery. You look like a lady and you act like one but you are in service."

Lady Maria looked delightfully flustered.

"I crave your pardon. I didn't mean to unsettle you. You may keep as many secrets as you want. Milady, I'm not an impetuous man but I know you are the woman I want as my wife. Will you marry me?"

"You told me at the folly that you didn't believe love was necessary for a marriage."

"I was a fool. I haven't been able to get you out of my thoughts. I've realized I can't marry anyone else. But you don't look happy. Have you changed your mind about me?"

Lady Maria shook her head.

"Then I've startled you with my proposal. You don't have to give me your answer right away. Come, let's talk about other things. Tell me about your childhood and your interests. Do you like to read? Paint? Sing?"

Daventon led her to a garden seat for which Lady Maria was thankful. She hadn't expected Gareth to propose; she had hoped he would, someday, but this was too sudden and unlike the stilted proposals of her other suitors which she had known how to decline without giving offense. Not that she wanted to turn down Gareth. Her heart had leaped at his offer but Gwen's words of caution, her own upbringing, and her terrible secret kept her from accepting right away.

Gareth subtly introduced topics that sparked her interest. When Gwen peeped over the hedge a quarter hour later, she found them in animated conversation about America. They didn't notice her and she resumed her post of sentry. But not for long. More people were coming into the garden and could wander into the lane. She returned to find Evenson and Lady Maria discussing geometry.

"That is based on the Equilateral Arch from Euclid's Elements," Mr. Evenson was saying, drawing a figure in the air.

"You will be surprised how geometry can be used in designing bonnets," Lady Maria answered, and rattled on about the intersection of a parabola.

Surprisingly, there was only admiration in Mr. Evenson's eyes; a member of the *ton* would have hastily retreated, branding Lady Maria a bluestocking.

"Gwen, I'm having such a nice time. Must we leave?" Lady Maria asked when Gwen drew nearer.

"I fear we must."

Daventon stood up and gave his hand to Lady Maria. "I look forward to our next meeting my lady...Milady," he said, raising her hand to his lips.

"That may not be possible," Gwen said. "I agreed to accompany Lady M.. Milady this one time. Even if no impropriety occurs, a clandestine meeting can ruin her good name."

"Gwen, can't we meet in the shop tomorrow? Who is to know?" asked Lady Maria.

"Adam will know," Gwen pointed out.

Lady Maria looked crushed. Daventon took her face in his hands and planted a chaste kiss on her forehead. "You know I want to marry you. Shall I call at Severn House for you? There cannot be anything improper in our meeting if I obtain permission to court you. Whom should I see?"

Lady Maria gazed at him mutely.

"Why are you silent? Is there any obstacle to my suit? You are not betrothed to another, I hope?"

"Me? What makes you ask that?"

"That is the only hurdle that can keep us apart."

"Gareth, I need some time to arrange matters," Lady Maria said and looked towards Gwen for help.

"Mr. Evenson, this is rather sudden for Lad...Milady. She needs some time. She'll write to you when she comes to a decision. You must not importune her until then. She won't be going to the shop from now on. If you have an urgent message, you may send it to Gwen Matthews at Severn House."

Daventon gave the directions of his new lodgings. Just then voices were heard coming up the lane. "Quick! Turn around and face the hedge!" Gwen hissed.

It was a boisterous group mouthing bawdy jests broken with raucous laughter. As soon as they went further away, Gwen took hold of Lady Maria's hand and, without waiting for the couple to indulge in farewells, hurried her out of the garden. Lord Daventon followed her with his eyes until she was out of sight.

So his love had a flair for geometry and was fiercely loyal to the memory of her parents. This had led her to Stubbs. He even had an inkling as to why she designed bonnets – he was sure the acclaimed Mme. Brigitte was a front– she wanted to feel independent. She was unique, indeed a diamond of the first water, an Incomparable, though the *ton* would condemn the very qualities that made her shine in his eyes.

Until now the women he had known were weak or frivolous. Even Aunt Nell had always depended on his father, and now on his opinions.

Lady Maria was not afraid to use her brain and had a strong will. She would come as an equal in their marriage. Unlike Lady Daventon who had retreated in the face of her husband's anger, and wallowed in her own pain, Lady Maria would fight for what she wanted.

He dared not think what she would do when she found out he was Lord Daventon and had kept her in the dark about his identity!

# Chapter 17

Eager to start living his dream, Nat Stevenson presented himself at the club at an early hour. He didn't have to wait for long. Lord Daventon summoned him to his room soon after breaking fast. "So Nat, what does a valet do? Do you know your duties?"

"My lord, I am here to serve you to your satisfaction. You won't have any cause for complaint. Your dressing room will always be in order, and I'll take good care of your clothes."

Lord Daventon didn't look impressed. "Any valet can do that. I want a good valet. Someone who keeps his master's secrets and treats his whims as commands."

Nat assured his lordship he could be as mute as a grave. Then his lordship gave him a letter, to be personally delivered by him. It was addressed to Milady Adam and he was to slip it under a locked door. The directions were to the shop near his old office!

That was the start to a most puzzling day.

Nat acquired modest lodgings in the name of Gareth Evenson and moved the earl's belonging into it. Apparently, they would be staying there though not for long because his lordship didn't want him to unpack much.

Why were they moving when an army of workers was sprucing up Daventon House? Mr. Meyers had already hired a butler and a housekeeper. They were engaging more staff. His lordship could have stayed on at the club and moved into Daventon House when it was ready. And why did he want to use an assumed name?

Nat reined in his thoughts. He was a valet, a trusted aid, and would obey his lordship's commands. It was not his place to speculate about them. Nat didn't see his master until the evening when he arrived in a hack and went straight into the tiny sitting room. He asked Nat to bring him his stationery. By a lucky chance, Nat had unpacked it.

He called Nat when the letter was finished. "Deliver this at Severn House," he said.

"Will you be going out again, my lord? Should I lay out evening clothes for you?" Nat asked, eager to start what he saw as the most exciting of his duties.

"I'll be attending to the post you picked up from Lord Barrington's," his master said, adding he would dine at home so would Nat bring something on his way back?

\*\*\*

Lady Maria was not particular about her supper, either. She picked at the roast duck until her grace had finished her portion, and accepted a tiny helping of the next course. After completion of the long-drawn-out meal, she accompanied her grace to the drawing room. It was the first evening Lady Severn had left her room since returning from Mayrick Manor.

"Are you finding the Season tedious, dear? You stayed home every evening. I hope you aren't unwell. Your color is rather high."

Lady Maria murmured that she was in good health. A footman came in with a letter on a tray. It had just been delivered.

"How unusual for a letter to be sent at this hour! It's from Lord Daventon. I hope it isn't bad news," Lady Severn said, opening the envelope.

As she read the letter, her expression changed to one of surprise, and then concern. She read it through and pursed her lips, and stared ahead of her.

"What is it, your grace?" Lady Maria asked.

"I don't know what to make of it. Have you met Lord Daventon?"

"No, your grace."

"Is it true that you don't want to marry him?"

"I can't marry him, your grace."

"Is anything amiss with the man?"

Blushing a deep red, Lady Maria hung her head. "N.no. You see, I never had any intention of marrying him!"

"Why did you agree? What were you planning to do? Leave him standing at the altar?"

Much to the duchess' surprise, Lady Maria nodded.

"He seems to know you don't want to marry him. He writes that he would be obliged if you will continue the engagement until the end of the Season. His mother and sister are coming up to London. It will be Lady Laura's first Season and for Lady Daventon, her first appearance in Society after so many years. Breaking the engagement will cause gossip and that will affect them. He will not hold you to the engagement after the Season unless you desire it."

Lady Maria waited for her grace to upbraid her. Instead, she said, "Maria, I will not deny I was looking forward to your nuptials with Lord Daventon. He seemed the perfect match for you. I can't agree more with him that a broken engagement will attract gossip that both our families can ill afford. If there is no other eligible match in the offing, I suggest you continue with the engagement until we return home. Of course, that will mean you will have to be seen in his company."

Lady Severn retired shortly afterwards. Lady Maria noticed the letter lying on the tray. She took it to her room and read it. It was a well-written letter, she had to concede, courteous and to the point. She couldn't help being impressed by the concern he showed towards his mother and sister.

How did he know she didn't want to marry him? Had Amy guessed and told him? It couldn't be. Amy was looking forward to her wedding with Lord Daventon. And then the truth struck her: Lord Daventon had seen her with Gareth that afternoon.

\*\*\*

The next morning brought a flood of callers. One reason was Lady Osbourne's poorly attended ball. Daughter of a wealthy cit, Heather had married Lord Osbourne, the bacon-brained third son of a viscount who spent more time in gaming holes than anywhere else. He had died within the year. The *ton* had expected Heather to fade away but the upstart wouldn't take the hint. She conducted events on par with other members of the *ton*. Her latest was a ball with musicians from Venice.

The other reason was Lady Daventon; word had spread that she was coming out of her self-imposed exile.

"I remember her from her comeout. She snared Edward Daventon easily enough though she wasn't anything out of the ordinary," said Lady Goodall and went on to describe the scandal, which her listeners lapped up.

Some scandals were like wine; they aged well.

Lord Hardwick came calling but no one paid him much attention. He bowed over Lady Maria's hand and invited her to ride in his new curricle. Lady Maria had little liking for him but thought it a good escape. Already the room was buzzing with conversation, some condoning and others criticizing Lady Daventon's behavior.

Lady Maria let herself be helped into the curricle. "Lord Hardwick, is this your new curricle? My memory must be serving me wrong but I remember it from an earlier outing."

"You have seen through my artifice, my lady. I hope you will not hold it against me."

"Not at all, my lord. It is a pleasant day to be outdoors."

Lord Hardwick was amongst her most deferential suitors but he gave her a surprisingly bold look. "The weather is indeed pleasant. I hear the Kensington

Gardens are looking their best. I was there last evening and saw a most interesting sight."

Lady Maria gave a tiny nod and looked away.

Lord Hardwick persisted. "Such affairs need finesse, my lady. Now if it was me, I wouldn't have exposed you to the public gaze. I have a well-appointed place for such assignations. You have only to say the word. Your betrothed needn't know."

"You are odious, sir. I insist you drive me back immediately!"

"If I don't, madam? Will you jump out? Believe me, that will cause a lesser scandal than Sweet Maria cavorting in a public place with a man!"

Lady Maria turned white. This was not the Lord Hardwick she had led with bonnet strings! Blood rushed to her face as he continued about his discreet liaisons with married women and widows. All he wanted was to meet her one time and she would have his silence, he gave his word as a gentleman. If she didn't, he would see to it that she was ruined. "Lord Daventon won't accept soiled goods, no one will, not even Hennicker. You have nothing to do that you haven't done before," he leered.

Instead of answering him, Lady Maria looked around for a way to escape. She spotted Lord Barrington driving up the street. He stood up in his curricle and bowed, intending to ride on but Lady Maria stopped him. "We are well met, my lord! I was planning on visiting with dear Amy. Will you please drive me to your townhouse?"

Lord Hardwick cut in. "Allow me, Lady Maria!"

Barrington was quick to note that Lady Maria didn't want Lord Hardwick to accompany her. He helped her down from the curricle. Lord Hardwick looked livid. He briefly tipped his hat and rode on.

"Has he been bothering you, Lady Maria?" Lord Barrington asked. "Do you really want to see Amy or shall I drive you home?"

"Please drive me home," Lady Maria said, putting up her parasol to shield her overheated face. On reaching Severn House, she tiptoed past the drawing room from which the hum of voices continued as before and went up to her room. There was no one in there; the maid had already picked it clean and Gwen was elsewhere, perhaps sitting in the housekeeper's room with her basket of mending.

Lady Maria lay down on the bed in her walking dress. Gwen would scold her for creasing it but that was a trivial matter. Her heart was going fast as if she had run a race. Her stays hurt and her head throbbed with the beginning of a headache.

What a coil! What should she do? She had always said that she didn't care if she caused a scandal. She had been prepared to leave Lord Daventon and to sail for America. She knew tongues would wag when she wed Evenson who wasn't a member of the *ton*.

But this was different. It cast a blemish on her character. It made her chaste meeting with the man she loved into something dirty, sordid. She could guess at the half truths Lord Hardwick would spread. A veiled innuendo here and there would have her name bandied about and in no time, she would become the social pariah. It would shatter Lady Severn. At one time she had wanted to throw convention into the duchess' face but now the very thought of it pained her.

When would Lord Hardwick strike?

They were going to Almack's and it being Wednesday, there would be dancing. From her second season on, the patronesses had given their nod for her to waltz. Emily Stewart, Lady Castlereagh had remarked that half the *ton* – the male half – wouldn't have it otherwise.

She prayed Lord Hardwick wouldn't ask her to dance.

***

Lady Maria chose to wear a sea blue gown made from fine Indian silk. It had a prim neckline at the front and plunged low at the back, the opening covered by a sheer fabric encrusted with diamantes. The long sleeves were of the same fabric. She wore a diamond choker and matching bracelets.

Rosie looked awestruck. "My lady, your gown is like the evening sky with the pretty stars twinkling in it."

Lady Maria knew she looked well. But there was only so much a fashionable gown could do. If Lord Hardwick chose to attack, it wouldn't save her reputation from being in shreds. Between her reputation and the gossamer thin fabric in her gown, the fabric was by far the stronger.

Lady Maria's dance card filled up fast and she breathed a little easier. However, when Lord Hardwick made his appearance at her side, she had one dance to spare. Relief washed over her as Lord Barrington shouldered his way through her crush of suitors. "Lady Maria! Have you saved me a dance? You promised me you would!"

She allowed him to scribble his name on the card. He proffered her arm. "Shall we take a turn around the room? You can point out the most interesting toilettes for Amy's benefit."

Lady Maria repressed a shudder as she walked away from Lord Hardwick. She could feel his eyes boring into her back and fervently wished her gown was made of holland or sackcloth rather than silk and net.

Lord Barrington kept up an inconsequential chatter and was relieved to see Lady Maria's face lose its marble-like rigidity. Lady Maria was betrothed to his best friend. He also liked her for her own sake. He didn't know why Hardwick was pestering her when she was already engaged but it was clear his attentions were unwelcome to her. He gallantly remained at her side until Lord Hardwick left the ball.

Lord Hardwick did not figure among the morning callers but was present at Lady Cynthia's soiree. Midway during the musical performance he slid into the seat beside Lady Maria. She managed to thwart his attempts at conversation and later, changed her seat. This drew a malevolent smile from him.

She called on Amy the next morning. Lord Barrington was also at home and gamely participated in their conversation about parasols and bonnets. Amy was delighted with him until he said it made no sense for women to use both bonnets and parasols.

Lord Barrington adroitly changed the topic. "Lady Maria, do you know Lady Laura and her aunt are arriving tomorrow? They were to go to Wrenrose directly but their plans are now changed because Daventon and his mother are also arriving in a day or two."

"Have you met Lady Laura?" Amy asked and answered her own question, "You couldn't have met her. James was telling me she had led a sheltered life. This is the first time she will be coming to London during the Season. She's lucky you are there to help her go about. Will you be calling on her tomorrow?"

Lord Barrington knew his wife's penchant for direct questions. Before she could probe further, he launched into a description of his Eton days with Daventon. His lordship's gentlemanly letter had impressed Lady Maria; she was very much interested in knowing more about his growing years. By the time she took leave of Amy, it was well-nigh over an hour.

Gwen had gone to the bonnet shop, to see how things were. She returned to find Lady Maria reading a letter. "Did Mr. Evenson send it?" she asked.

"No. This is his old letter."

"Your visit to Lady Barrington has agreed with you. You were not your usual self these last days."

"Gwen, Amy was telling me about Lord Daventon. He is wonderfully kind to his mother and sister. Do you think it will be the right thing to call on his sister tomorrow? She is come up from the country and this will be her first Season."

"Why? Lord Daventon has written that he is breaking the engagement, hasn't he?"

"He wants the pretense to continue. What can be more natural than calling upon Lady Laura and shepherding her through the Season? With the scandal attached to her mother, it will not be easy for her. Lady Goodall and the like will give her a miserable time."

"What about Mr. Evenson? Are you going to tell him who you are? He has a right to know."

"He'll know soon enough. Gwen, what do you suggest I wear for the duke's reception?" Lady Maria asked. The Duke of Mercham had stayed her most loyal beau until her engagement to Lord Daventon. On the very next day, he had proposed to and been accepted by the youngest daughter of an impoverished earl. The reception was to introduce his affianced bride to Society.

"You look lovely in anything, my dear. How about the damask gown? Or the lustre one? It is newly come."

"I'll wear the damask. It becomes me well."

And it did. Lady Maria had seldom looked lovelier. The gown was of a green shade with a subtle floral pattern woven into the fabric. An empire waistline, long sleeves and a square neckline accentuated her trim figure. Her necklace, bracelet, and drop earrings were of gold and emerald.

Lord Hardwick stood in the shadows and watched her mingle with the other guests. The Duke of Mercham raised her gloved hands to his lips. Lord Hardwick wasn't given to much thinking. He had never been popular with the ladies unless it was with the demi- monde where his purse eased his way. The evening he had seen Lady Maria in Kensington Garden, he was in a group of six young men belonging to noble families, and three out-of- work actresses. When he had passed the shrubbery, he had recognized Lady Maria's maid. Behind her stood Lady Maria close to a man. Their backs were turned to him but he knew it was Lady Maria and the circumstances spoke of intrigue.

He had long aspired for her hand, not because he was in love with her, she was too serious for him, but she was a matrimonial prize. If he won her, he would win the admiration of all women, and stand tall among men.

Seeing her in a compromising position, he had felt a wave of disgust, as if she had betrayed him by stepping down from a pedestal. She owed him reparation. He would treat her like a bit of muslin for that is what she was. He had threatened her and enjoyed her squirming in his power. After three days, his passion had given way to cunning.

He managed to corner her before supper was announced. "Lady Maria, please forgive my boorishness. It was naught but a lover's disappointment. Will you do me the honor of becoming my wife?"

"Are you in your cups, sir? I'm betrothed to Lord Daventon."

"You must break the engagement and accept my offer. It is that or scandal. I will give you time until Lady Malloy's ball. If you don't do it, I shall pay a visit of a private nature to Lord Daventon and I can assure you he will break the engagement."

Lady Maria gave him a contemptuous look. It brought forth a smirk. "I would prefer you to break the engagement. I don't want any scandal to be attached to my future wife."

Hardwick left soon after.

The duke had arranged for fire-eaters and acrobats to perform on his lawns. Lackeys served a steady stream of small, exotic courses to the guests as they remained seated. But Lady Maria couldn't enjoy the evening.

Face to face with Lord Hardwick, she had seen the malicious face of the *ton*. Barely hidden by the polite talk was malice, and no mercy would be shown if she didn't play by the rules.

# Chapter 18

Lady Laura didn't know how she felt. And that wasn't new.

She could never decide who was luckier: she whose mother hadn't loved her enough to stay or Janet, the maid, an orphan whose mother had loved her until her last breath.

Was it a good thing to have a father who loved her but often forgot her existence? Would life have been better if her mother had stayed with them and her father had left?

The only thing she was sure about was Gareth, the brother she loved and who loved her back and cared for her.

Now he had brought an upheaval in her life. They had come to London and their mother was joining them. She was to have a Season, perhaps be presented in Court, attend balls and such.

Lady Helena was delighted. "You will make a splendid match, my dear," she prophesied. But all Lady Laura could think of was the mother she knew only from the ink-stained portrait in the attic, and who had eyes as wide and grey as her own.

Laura was filled with conflicting emotions. Helpless love clashed with resentment for her mother, and fear of scandal engulfed both. A scandal so big it had even infringed upon her childhood in the country.

Lady Helena misunderstood her silence and tried to reassure her. "You can hold your own among the other girls. You have received a good education. You play the piano and the harp, and have a sweet singing voice. Thanks to Lydia, you know the latest dance steps. And you don't need to be worried about your wardrobe. Gareth will have taken steps to replenish it."

It would have helped if Gareth was there to prepare her for the meeting. He understood her. The only silver lining was they were not receiving callers. Aunt Nell had decided they would wait until Gareth and Lady Daventon arrived from Wrenrose.

And now there was a caller! And the butler had already shown her in!

"Aunt Nell, you must tell Lady Maria we are not at home!"

"That would be downright rude, my dear. Come, there's nothing wrong with your gown. Emma can redo your hair if you wish though I must say you look very fetching as you are."

With these words of encouragement, Lady Helena led her into the drawing room.

Lady Maria stood up when they came in. "Lady Helena, I know you aren't receiving callers yet but…"

"You are family, dear, or soon to be! Pray come and sit with me!"

Lady Laura seated herself across from her aunt. She greeted Lady Maria and answered her polite inquiries in a civil manner. Lady Helena kept up the conversation with inquiries about the duchess. This led to some fond recollections of her own childhood, and the friendship her mother and her grace had enjoyed.

All through this, Lady Maria was conscious of Lady Laura. It was like she was seeing her own self. Not her grown up self but the little girl who had built a wall of reserve around her. Laura was sitting ramrod straight with her hands folded in her lap. It was obvious she had been well trained in posture and deportment. The curling fringe of her eyelashes guarded her expression.

A wave of empathy swept through Lady Maria. Laura is so fragile, she thought. A wrong word will shatter her and she's so strong no one will know! That's why Lord Daventon is so concerned about her.

"We had several invitations waiting when we arrived," said Lady Helena.

"Lady Malloy's ball is eagerly awaited. You must attend it."

Lady Helena found the invitation. "That's only two days away. I'm afraid we can't attend. We came up to London at short notice and the country, as you know, lags sadly behind in fashion."

"That can soon be remedied," said Lady Maria. "Modistes always stock gowns that can be altered within the day. They might not be of the first stare but will do very well for now. Shall I ask my modiste to send over a selection?"

"Here? Will she do that?"

"She will when she knows it is for ladies recently come up for the Season."

"Why is that?" Lady Laura asked.

Lady Maria smiled warmly at her. "That's because she can get more orders from you!"

The modiste sent over two dozen gowns. They were of the latest designs and brought a sparkle to Lady Laura's eyes. Lady Maria watched as she exhibited excellent taste in picking out colors and designs best suited to her. She also had a mind of her own. Though her aunt wanted her to stick to the conventional white, she said she looked a fright in it. For herself, Lady Helena chose from shades of grey and mauve as she was in half-mourning for her brother.

A satisfactory selection was made within the hour. The seamstress who had brought the gowns took their measurements. She assured them two gowns would be delivered the very same evening, and the others on the morrow.

"What about Mama? Do you think she will have something suitable for Lady Malloy's ball?" Lady Laura asked, and colored.

"Everyone will be agog to see her because of her circumstances. If she wears something breathtaking, they will focus on that," Maria said.

Lady Laura's eyes widened and she looked at Lady Maria with dawning respect.

"I've tested it. Nothing beats Scandal like Fashion unless it is a Bigger Scandal. So if Lady Daventon has not had the time or opportunity of repairing her wardrobe, you must not attend Lady Malloy's ball."

"I don't care about balls and what people say!"

Lady Maria felt a surge of affection. Laura was like her, fiercely loyal to her mother which did her great credit because she had barely known her.

"Lady Laura, there are many ways of showing your disdain. One is to follow their rules so well that they start emulating you."

"Is that what you do?"

"I'm called Sweet Maria and often held up as an example of model behavior."

"So you can do no wrong in the eyes of the *ton*?"

"Alas, only royalty can do no wrong. By my circumspect behavior, I have Society's indulgence and favor. For now, at least."

Lady Maria's open manner captivated Laura and very soon they were on first name basis. A shopping expedition was planned for the next day. By the time Maria left, Laura had confided some of her fears in her. She had even accepted to wear white as it was her first Season.

***

Except for Lord Hardwick's ominous threat which Maria chose to ignore, the next day dawned bright and clear. She called at Daventon House after breaking fast. Laura was waiting for her. She was dressed in a paisley walking dress trimmed with petit point. It was the gown they had selected the previous day.

"The dress becomes you very well. Now, you must wear this bonnet," Lady Maria said, showing her the wide-brimmed creation she had brought.

"Oh, it's beautiful!"

"It's a gift to celebrate your first shopping expedition. Are you ready? Lady Helena?"

"Both of you go, dear. I want to spend some time with the housekeeper."

"We'll take Gwen along; she can serve as chaperon. Laura, let me tie that bonnet again. It will look better with the ribbons tied below the chin."

Their first stop was at the dressmaker's. Fortunately, she had a white gown that suited Laura to perfection. She also had many other dresses and accessories in the latest styles. Between Lady Maria's advice and Laura's own good taste, they managed to pick up a heap of clothes.

They followed this up with purchasing trinkets and pretty shoes, and the most essential item that bespoke a lady, gloves. A footman followed them, efficiently transferring the packages into the carriage.

Lady Laura took in the sights. So that was Jackson's club? And the young man affecting that mincing walk – what was it called? The Bond Street Roll? Didn't he look absurd? He brought to mind a juggler's monkey!

"We must stop at Gunter's," Lady Maria said, expertly shepherding Laura through the people thronging the pavements. Some were there to shop but most were there to be seen. They greeted Lady Maria effusively and she introduced Laura to them. By evening everyone would know that Lady Daventon's daughter was in London.

Maria ordered ices for Laura and Gwen and a sorbet for herself. Laura looked happy as she savored the first ice of her life. "I hope my brother doesn't regret giving me a free hand. He is likely to drown in the bills!" she said, spooning the last of the ice and looking around happily.

"I don't think he will complain. Lord Barrington was telling me he loves you very much."

"I'm so glad you are to be my sister! When Aunt Nell told me about you, I thought you would be cold and haughty."

Gwen shot Lady Maria a worried look. What was she doing? Why was she befriending Lord Daventon's sister when her engagement would come to an end?

As soon as they returned home, Rosie handed Lady Maria a letter. A messenger had brought it.

"It must be from Mr. Evenson," Gwen said.

It was from Lord Hardwick. Lady Maria turned pale as she read it. The next morning she penned two letters: one to Mr. Evenson and the other to Lord Daventon.

# Chapter 19

After his meeting with Lady Maria in Kensington Garden, Lord Daventon had hoped she would send him a message soon, and arrange to see him. The sooner he told her who he was the better. When Lady Daventon and Laura came to town, he would have to attend *ton* parties. It would be nigh impossible to keep up the pretense.

But two days later, Lady Daventon summoned him to Wrenrose. She wrote that Betty and her assistants had proved to be most efficient. She had enough gowns to tide over for a few days. Betty had proclaimed her Paris gowns not outdated at all. In fact, they were a la mode, and superior to what the London dressmakers created. As Laura was of her height, and slender, they would do very well for her. She wanted to start for London at the earliest. Dearest Laura and Lady Helena need not come to Wrenrose. She would be at Daventon House to welcome them!

Daventon returned to Wrenrose, expecting his mother would be ready to start for London the very next day. However, the preparations and the packing took longer than expected. In addition, he had to give his attention to the repair work lest his mother overtire herself. It was four days before they returned to London.

Four interminable days! Every moment his thoughts flitted to Milady, My Lady, with the fervent wish that she didn't send a note to his lodgings in his absence. And an ardent prayer that he should get the opportunity to speak to her before she knew of his deception.

Having made an early start, they reached Daventon House by eleven o'clock.

Lady Daventon put on a bright smile though her hand in his was icy cold. Inclining her head graciously to the servants lined up, she greeted Lady Helena. Then she looked at Lady Laura and held open her arms. Lady Laura went to her. The servants slipped away. Lady Helena dabbed at her eyes as Lord Daventon held his mother and sister close for a long moment.

Gareth said, "Mother, you must be tired from the journey. Laura, why don't you take Mother to her room and help her settle in?"

After they left, he turned to his aunt. "Laura is looking well. I feared she would be annoyed with me for not preparing her for the visit."

"You must thank Lady Maria. She has been most kind to Laura. Not only has she helped her with her clothes, which you know Laura doesn't care much about, she has showed her genuine affection, treating her like the sister she will soon be. You have made a good choice, Gareth. Maria has a beautiful heart."

"How did Lady Maria come to be here? Did you invite her?"

"She called on her own. We didn't even have the knocker up."

Puzzling over the matter, Lord Daventon went to the rooms he had hired, to see if there was a message from Milady waiting for him.

There was and it made no sense.

*While I am honored by your regard and your marriage proposal, I must decline. I am the recipient of another Proposal that I must accept. I have come to believe you were right in saying that Love cannot be the basis of a Marriage.*

*I trust you are the gentleman I believe you to be and will destroy my letter after reading it.*

*Milady.*

"When did this come?" he asked Nat.

"A footman brought it an hour ago, my lord."

Nat stole a glance at his lordship; he looked like he had received a blow. Gareth dropped into a chair and read the letter again. He tugged at his neckcloth which made Nat wince. Then he ran impatient fingers through his hair, causing them to fall in unruly disarray.

"My lord?"

His lordship recollected himself and stood up. "Nat, I'll be staying at Daventon House. So shall you. Settle with the landlord and move our things.

Lord Daventon went to his club. It being early in the day yet, he found a quiet corner. Once again he read Lady Maria's message. What did it mean? When he had written to her grace, breaking the engagement, he was sure Milady would receive him with the happy news that she was free to marry him.

Who had proposed to her now? He knew she was always neck deep in proposals so it could be anyone. He thought she loved him, Gareth. She had seemed so sincere, so open about her love. Why had she accepted someone else? Dash it! He wouldn't stand by and let this happen.

*Love is a quagmire and you are caught. Caught the same way your father was!*

Someone pulled a chair and sat down uninvited. "I'm Lord Hardwick. I inherited from my uncle a year ago. I've never had the honor of meeting you in person but I know about you. You are honorable and a stickler for propriety."

Inwardly fuming at the intrusion, Lord Daventon barely touched the proffered hand and stood up to leave.

"Don't leave, my lord. I have come to speak about Lady Maria. She is not fit for you. Last week I saw her in Kensington Garden. She was with a ..."

Daventon's fist cut him short. It also cut his lip, and perhaps broke his nose.

Hardwick whimpered. "I have your interests at heart, my lord. I told Lady Maria she must break ..."

This time there was no doubt about it. Lord Hardwick would have to make up a story that would explain his crooked nose for life. That would be later. For now, Lord Daventon towered over him, making him tell all.

So that was it! Hardwick had seen Milady and recognized her and was blackmailing her. For the sake of her reputation, she had accepted to marry him.

Landing Hardwick one parting kick where it would hurt him the most, Daventon went home. He needed to freshen up before presenting himself at Severn House, at least for the sake of the duchess.

Nat was waiting for him. He had brought his bags from the lodgings and was now lovingly brushing a riding coat. Daventon washed his face and picked up a hairbrush. Nat was immediately at his side. "Allow me, my lord."

"Nat, I'm perfectly capable of combing my hair. I'm also in a hurry. I'll tell you what. You may lay out my clothes for the evening. My aunt tells me we are attending Lady Malloy's ball."

A footman scratched the door. A letter had come for his lordship in the morning but he had left before it could be brought to him. Lord Daventon would have flung it aside but it was from Severn House; Lady Maria had sent it.

To Nat's dismay, once again his lordship dropped into a chair and looked shattered. Before he could do damage to his fresh neckcloth or rumple his hair, Nat asked, "Can I be of service, my lord?"

"No, Nat. I will know soon enough what this means."

Five minutes later he was at Severn House, demanding to see Lady Maria. The butler led him to the morning room and announced him. Daventon went in and closed the door on his interested countenance. Propriety be dammed! He had much to say to Milady – Lady Maria – none of which was for public consumption.

Dressed in a striped dimity gown, Lady Maria looked cool and poised. Until she saw who her visitor was. "Mr. Evenson!" she said, her voice faint, and a lacy handkerchief to her lips.

Lord Daventon made a leg. "Gareth Evenson at your service, my lady. Come to offer my felicitations."

Lady Maria recovered. "It was not well done to gain entry into my house under a false name. I'm expecting a visit from Lord Daventon. Pray leave, sir!"

"I thought you loved me. But it was all a game, wasn't it? A lady playing at being a commoner, and toying with the feelings of whoever caught her fancy! Was I the only one, or were there more?"

"You are impertinent, sir! I can have you evicted."

"Call your lackeys then."

Lady Maria came to stand in front of him. "Mr. Evenson, I was not toying with your feelings. Some things are not meant to be. Pray don't create a scene."

"Why are you expecting Lord Daventon? He is prepared to end the engagement."

"How do you know this? Did Lord Daventon write that letter on your account? What did you say to him?" Lady Maria asked, alarm writ large on her face.

"You needn't worry, my love. Your Lord Daventon knew all the time. You see, I'm Lord Daventon. Evenson is one of my titles. I thought you wanted a love match and sent that letter. Free of the engagement, I expected you would accept me as Gareth Evenson. But you refused me."

"I refused Mr. Evenson, not you."

Lord Daventon held up the letter his footman had given him. "What is the meaning of this?"

"It is clear enough, my lord. I have asked you to reconsider your decision about ending our engagement. I have expressed my willingness to marry you."

"*I shall be honored to become your countess. There appears to be a misunderstanding. You may rest assured I have not formed any other attachment. Lady Maria, this* letter exposes you. You turned me down because you preferred a title."

"I turned you down? I agreed to wed you, my lord. Are you not Lord Daventon?"

"I'm Lord Daventon and you know what I mean. You accepted to marry me though you love Mr. Evenson, and that I cannot forgive."

"My lord, in that case, please consider our engagement at an end."

She inclined her head and made to sweep past him but he imprisoned her wrist. "Our engagement is not at an end! I will marry you, not for love but to save your reputation. Hardwick saw us together and threatens to slander you."

Lady Maria snatched her hand free. Eyes flashing fire, she flounced out of the room and walked straight into Gwen.

When Lord Daventon had shut the door completely instead of leaving it open by the few inches that propriety demanded, the butler had alerted Gwen. Gwen was alarmed, more so as the engagement was to come to an end. She stood outside the door, preparing to knock when the door opened and Lady Maria rushed out. Gwen saw Gareth Evenson behind her and went in.

"Sir, what did you tell Lady Maria? Why is she upset?"

"Lady Maria? You mean Milady."

"Is that why you came here as Lord Daventon? You are fortunate her grace is not yet down!"

Rather wearily, Daventon said, "I'm Lord Daventon. Gareth is my name and Evenson is a title I inherited from my uncle."

"But it is not the title you use, my lord. Had you introduced yourself as Lord Daventon, my lady wouldn't have suffered so much."

"Lady Maria suffering? She turned down Evenson this morning and broke her engagement with Lord Daventon just now!"

Gwen paled. "I hope she doesn't make up her mind to sail to America."

In an instant, Daventon's anger vanished. "Gwen, you must help me win her back. It doesn't matter whether she accepts me as Milady or Lady Maria but I can't lose her."

Lady Severn walked in on the astounding sight of Gwen having a tête-à-tête with Lord Daventon. Blushing to the roots of her hair, Gwen bowed herself out. Lord Daventon engaged in pleasantries with her grace as long as he could and made his escape. Lady Severn sent for Gwen, for an explanation.

"Your grace, Lord Daventon called on Lady Maria. They had an argument."

"Maria doesn't want to marry him and Daventon is prepared to end the engagement. What is there to argue?"

"She wants to marry him but she's angry, your grace," Gwen said, gripping the end of a chair. Haltingly, without disclosing about the bonnets and the misadventure with Stubbs, Gwen told the duchess that Lady Maria and Lord Daventon had met and fallen in love without knowing each other's identity.

"Now that they know, where is the problem? You say they love each other."

"Lady Maria is hurt and angry. I think she's feeling deceived."

"I can't blame her. I wouldn't have pegged Daventon to be the sort who would go about under a false name."

"He says it wasn't false. He was using a title he inherited from his uncle."

"Evenson?"

"Yes, your grace."

"What name was Lady Maria using?"

Gwen colored and remained silent.

"Ah, another secret you will guard with your life. I fail to understand why Lady Maria is upset when she herself has exercised the same deception."

"It was a misunderstanding, your grace. Neither of them intended to deceive."

"Well, I don't understand the misunderstanding. What should we do now?"

"We should help them come together, your grace. They are perfect for each other!"

# Chapter 20

Lady Maria spent the rest of the day in her room, sketching. Gwen left her to it; she was too busy answering Lady Daventon, Lady Severn, and Lady Helena. The ladies were determined to bring Lord Daventon and Lady Maria together.

Lady Daventon was so taken up in the matrimonial project of her son to the woman he loved that she forgot to be nervous about the ball. "We must contrive to send them in the same carriage. Helena and I will come in your carriage."

"What about Laura?"

"Let's do it this way. Laura and you will go with her grace. I'll go with Gareth and Maria, and pretend to sleep!" Lady Helena said.

After agreeing on this and other strategies, the conspirators separated, to get some rest before the ball.

Lord Daventon spent the better part of the day in his study. He emerged when his mother summoned him to join them for tea.

"Gareth, have you seen the gowns Mama brought with her? They are magnificent! I wish I could wear one of them to the ball."

"Why don't you?" Gareth asked mechanically.

"None of them is white. Lady Maria told me I must wear white, at least for the first few balls. She says appearances are everything. And gowns matter."

"Bonnets. Bonnets matter, too," Gareth said, a smile lightening his face.

"That's true. She gifted me a bonnet and it transformed my face. Mother, you will love Maria. She is so clever and obliging."

"I'm sure I'll love her, dear. I've taken her advice about my gown, haven't I?"

Gareth was surprised. "Mother, I thought you hadn't met her."

"I haven't, dear. She told Laura I must wear a breathtaking gown to the ball. Fortunately, Betty is most skilled and she has equipped me with a suitable wardrobe," said Lady Daventon, smiling brightly at Gareth, who guessed how frightened she actually was.

He laced his fingers with hers. "Mother, you have many friends who will be delighted to see you again."

Lady Helena came in. "Dear Catherine, you needn't worry in the least. Lady Severn is your champion, and many follow her lead."

After tea, Daventon went up to his room and found Nat as nervous as a debutante. He had laid out three sets of evening wear. For once, Daventon was in a quandary about what he should wear. Was Lady Maria a connoisseur of male fashion, too? Finally, he chose a snow-white shirt with ruffles, a waistcoat of muted silk, and a grey double-breasted tailcoat. Nat lamented his lordship did not possess a pair of mustard pantaloons and sighed when he chose to wear black breeches.

It was well-nigh an hour before his mother, aunt, and sister were ready to leave.

"I'm to escort three lovely ladies. Laura, I would never have expected you to clean up so well!"

Laura made a face and punched him in the arm. "I wanted to thank you for the pearls and the flowers but now I shall not!" she declared.

Lady Daventon smiled at this display of sibling love. "Gareth, it was thoughtful of you to select presents for your sister. Did you get something for Lady Maria, too? We are stopping at Severn House so that I can become acquainted with her. We will make our entrance at the ball as one party. Lady Severn wishes it and I think it a splendid idea."

As their carriage pulled into the driveway of Severn House, Daventon's heart started racing. Though he had seen Lady Maria only a few hours ago, he was eager to see her again. He only hoped she didn't refuse to see him!

Lady Maria and the duchess were waiting for them. Lady Maria gave him a civil greeting and was led away by Lady Daventon to sit with her. Lady Laura and Lady Helena joined them, leaving Daventon to carry on a stilted conversation with her grace. What made it so difficult was Lady Severn kept talking about Lady Maria. She even drew his attention to how well she looked!

Daventon found it impossible to draw his eyes away from her. She was strikingly beautiful in a burgundy-colored gown. He knew she was aware of his regard because she looked their way whenever Lady Severn spoke to her. But she had no problem looking away again.

"We should be leaving now," Lady Severn said, and sent word for the carriages. His mother, chatting gaily with her grace and clasping Laura's hand, walked to the ducal carriage. Not believing his luck, Daventon handed Lady Maria into his carriage. Then he helped Lady Helena in and sat down beside Lady Maria. The carriage started and Lady Helena closed her eyes.

"Lady Maria?"

But Lady Maria was most interested in looking out. One would think this was her first visit to London! Lord Daventon folded his arms across his chest and leaned back. With his face in the shadow, he watched her though half-closed eyes.

What an enchanting profile she had! The nape of her neck itself was a work of art. While she continued to look out of the window, Daventon studied her charming coiffure and the play of one long curl against her shoulder. He was rewarded for his patience. Lady Maria looked in his direction. Perhaps his continued silence had made her curious. Finding him in seeming repose, she let her eyes roam freely over him. The minx! How well she had pretended to be indifferent.

His good humor restored, Daventon let the charade continue until they reached their destination, which wasn't that long. He stepped down with alacrity and handed his aunt down. Lady Maria extended a prim hand; he helped her down and, ignoring her indignant look, held on to it.

Lady Daventon beamed approvingly as they joined the long receiving line. Daventon freed Lady Maria's hand and offered her his arm. She laid decorous fingers on it and looked up at him. "Lady Daventon looks well. We must see to it that nothing spoils her evening."

Daventon knew their entrance would cause a flutter, there would be gossip, and the old scandal would be dished out again. But he was confident his mother would weather it. She was not the woman who had lived tremulously alone, longing for her family, waiting for her husband to call her back but one who had discovered her own strength, and it showed in her bearing.

"Lady Maria, I thank you for your kindness to Laura and your concern for my mother," Daventon answered.

Lady Maria was looking around, a tiny crease on her forehead. Daventon leaned closer. "Hardwick is at home. He won't be sticking his nose into anyone's business. I broke it."

Lady Severn and Lady Helena were announced, followed by Lady Daventon and Lady Laura, and Lord Daventon and Lady Maria.

Heads swiveled, and conversation dropped. Curious eyes raked them, going past Lady Daventon and settling on Lord Daventon and his affianced bride. No one had seen them together until now. It was rumored that the engagement was broken. Lady Goodall asserted it was a sham and had not existed in the first place.

Lord Barrington detached himself from a group of young men. "Gareth! Good to see you! Lady Maria! I must tell Amy how beautiful you look this evening. On second thoughts, it would be better you called 'cause I won't be able to answer her questions."

Daventon introduced him to his mother, aunt, and sister. Barrington recalled a young earl who was making his first appearance of the Season and asked to be permitted to introduce him to Lady Laura.

Lady Maria's usual court surrounded her, and before Daventon realized, her dance card was almost full. He hastily scribbled his name against the only available dance, a quadrille, and walked away, leaving her with the men who insisted on plying her with lemonade and regaling her with gossip.

Daventon moved to one side of the ballroom and was joined by several gentlemen he was acquainted with. They congratulated him on the brilliant match he had made and hoped Lady Maria would succeed in bringing him to London more often.

"Besotted, aren't we?" Barrington murmured, as Daventon's eyes followed Lady Maria. She had left her admirers and was introducing Lady Laura to the other debutantes.

The first dance was a country dance, and he was partnering Laura. This was the first time she would be dancing in public; there had been no village assemblies and country parties to prepare her for a Season.

"Imagine you are dancing with me at Daventon Hall," he murmured, leading her to the dance floor.

"If I do that, I'll have a fit of the giggles! You are not to worry. Mama made me practice my steps. I shall do very well except for the waltz which I will sit out."

Daventon found her true to her word. She executed the steps faultlessly. He was proud of her, he could already see she stood out among the debutantes, her manner being a blend of freshness and poise. After the dance, he handed her to Lord Emsworth and walked over to Lord Barrington.

"Whom are you partnering with for the other dances?" Barrington inquired.

"Lady Maria for one dance."

"It is *de rigueur* to also dance with females who are not related by ties of blood or betrothed to us," Lord Barrington intoned.

Daventon shrugged but made no move towards the array of women who, while talking to each other, darted hopeful glances at the men approaching them. The next dance was announced. Barrington escorted his partner to the floor who was a rather plain debutante.

Lady Maria's partner was handsome and she looked at him with seeming adoration. For the next dance she had the Honorable Eliot King. Did she know he was a rake, and no woman was safe with him? Why was she bestowing him a sweet smile?

And did she have to dance every dance?

He approached her with a rather surly expression for the quadrille. "My dance, I believe."

Lady Maria made an elaborate show of studying her dance card. "So it appears to be!"

They took their places and bowed. Lady Maria smiled brightly. "You don't look happy, milord. Is anything amiss?"

"You, on the contrary, appear delighted. I take it your partners pleased you."

The dance commenced and they separated. When they came together again, Lady Maria said, "You are ungallant, sir. I thought Laura danced exceptionally well."

Daventon's face broke into a smile. She had been watching him, too! He touched a finger to her cheek and she raised her face. Then she spun to face another partner. From then on, Daventon enjoyed every minute of the dance and thought it came to an end too soon.

"The next is the supper dance. Who is your partner?" he asked Lady Maria.

"Lord Barrington."

Daventon escorted Lady Maria to Lord Barrington. "James, would you mind sitting out this dance?"

"That would be rude. A lady may plead a torn flounce but a gentleman is obliged to keep his word."

Lady Maria fluttered her eyelashes. "My lord, you make dancing with me sound a chore."

"I crave your pardon, my lady, if I gave the impression. It was exceedingly ham-fisted of me. My words were meant for Lord Daventon. He must take the trouble of securing a dance if he desires one!"

Lord Daventon flicked open Lady Maria's dance card. He struck off Barrington's name and scrawled his own. "Thank you, James, for pointing me in the right direction. I hope you are satisfied that the proprieties have been observed."

"I'm afraid I have torn a flounce! How exceedingly remiss of me!" Lady Maria said with a straight face.

Barrington burst out laughing. Lord Daventon gave Lady Maria an indulgent smile, and his arm. "There is nothing to do for it but to sit the dance out. Shall we repair to the garden?"

After the confines of the ballroom, the garden was a welcome change. The air was perfumed with the fragrance of flowers, and the moon was full. Colored lanterns hung from tree branches. A few other couples were also outside. Lord Daventon escorted Lady Maria to a garden bench that was close enough to the well-lit path not to be considered improper.

Lady Maria spread her skirts elegantly which necessarily put a distance between them. Lord Daventon rested his arm on the back of the bench. It did not touch Lady Maria for she was a lady born and bred, and sat ramrod straight. Lord Daventon's lips twitched when she discreetly arched her feet under the gown. They must be hurting from all the dancing.

"Remove them. Who is to know?" he said.

Lady Maria shot him an indignant look.

"Milady would have."

"Much you know about Milady!"

"She doesn't care about convention. In fact, the first time I saw her was in a London street, paying homage to the sun."

"Milady wouldn't be allowed to attend Lady Malloy's ball. Neither would Gareth Evenson."

"Is that why you declined his proposal? Or was Hardwick the reason?"

"Hardwick threatened to expose me this evening and had the temerity to send me a very nasty letter. But I knew he did not have the gumption to carry out his threat."

"So I was right. You did choose a title over love. Sweet Maria did not care to lose her position among the *haute ton*. She would rather wear shoes that pinch her feet than remove them."

"Talking of shoes, the shoe fits *you*, my lord. *You* chose a title over love. By some means you discovered I was a lady and my grandmother was a duchess. You offered marriage to Lady Maria, not to Milady."

Lord Daventon groaned inwardly. Now he was in the suds! How did she find out? Was it Barrington?

As if reading his thoughts, Lady Maria said, "I spent an afternoon with Amy and Lord Barrington. They spoke at length about you. Lord Barrington used your given name. I was surprised that the Gareth to whom I had lost my heart had so much in common with Lord Daventon. Both had the same blue eyes, a cleft in the chin, dark hair, and were of the same height. They were knowledgeable about geometry. Family concerns often took them away from London. I compared the note you had sent me and the letter you wrote her grace. You will make a poor counterfeiter, my lord. While you altered your writing in the note you sent me, I traced the same strokes easily enough."

"I did not turn away from you lightly."

"You said there were those you had to consider above your own needs. After I met Laura, I understood your need to protect her. Why didn't you trust me? You could have told me all. I would have waited until Laura was wed."

"I'm sorry. Mine was not the intention to cause you hurt. I distrusted love, not you."

"And now?"

"I cannot live without your love. Lady Maria, will you accept to be my wife?"

Lady Maria looked at him with laughter in her eyes. "I believe we are betrothed, my lord. Unless you mean to jilt me and cause scandal."

"Do you think it will cause scandal if I propose to you on my knees?"

"It will most certainly attract attention, my lord. We have had a surfeit of unwanted attention, have we not?"

Lord Daventon raised her hand to his lips. "Did you suffer much as a child?"

Lady Maria rested her cheek against it for a moment. "I did. Oh yes, I did. It made me into an exemplary child. It also made me dread attention of any kind."

"My proposal will have to wait till tomorrow then. May I call at eleven o'clock?"

Lady Maria assented. Together they returned to the ball. Supper had just been announced but there were those who examined them closely as they came in. Seeing Lady Maria's coiffure and my lord's neckcloth unmolested, they turned their attention elsewhere to satisfy their craving for a morsel of Scandal.

# Chapter 21

The very air of Severn House was heavy with anticipation.

Rosie had her face glued to an upstairs window. The butler found reasons to stand at the front door. Cook had baked more batches of scones than were required for a houseful of guests.

Lady Maria had let her grace know his lordship would call, and also that he wanted to make a formal proposal for her hand. Her grace had told her dresser, and now everyone down to the scullery maid awaited his coming.

For they had keenly felt it when other servants had remarked that his lordship evinced little interest in courting their mistress.

Lord Daventon arrived on the dot. Before he could say anything, the butler took his greatcoat and led him to the library. Rosie was hovering in the passage. She tittered and opened the door to the library, and the butler shut it behind his lordship.

Lady Maria rose from the sofa and came forward. "You are punctual, my lord," she said and gave him her hand to kiss. Lord Daventon did not take it. He thrust his hand into one pocket after another. Then he started patting his waistcoat.

"What can be of such import to make you look flustered, my lord?"

"A poem. Amy had told me poems written in their honor please women above anything. I stayed up half the night trying to find words rhyming with Maria. The poem is not much by way of a literary effort but I thought it would serve as a romantic gesture. I was planning on asking you to burn it after you read it! Plague take Nat! He made me change my waistcoat thrice. It must have remained in another waistcoat."

Lady Maria succeeded in keeping a straight face. "I know you are no artist. It appears you are no poet either. What talent do you possess, my lord?"

Lord Daventon lowered himself elegantly on one knee and took Lady Maria's hands in his. "Only one talent, my lady. Of choosing the woman who suits me best. Will you marry me, Milady? I love you so much. Will you accept my suit, Lady Maria?"

Lady Maria thought to make a jest or keep his lordship kneeling for a little longer. But his earnest tone and the love shining in his eyes undid her. "Yes! Oh yes, my lord! I shall be your wife!" she said, tears pricking her eyes.

Lord Daventon rose to his feet and drew Lady Maria into his arms. She raised her face to his, and his eyes lingered on the petal soft lips parted to receive his kiss.

A knock on the door drew them apart. It was followed by a louder knock and some coughing.

"Come in," Lady Maria called, decorously seated away from Lord Daventon.

It was Rosie. Blushing and giggling, she informed they had callers and her grace wanted them to join her. Much to Lord Daventon's annoyance, she stood by the open door, waiting to follow them.

After an hour of making polite conversation, Lord Daventon stood up. "Lady Maria, shall we go?" he asked, and explained for everyone's benefit he was taking Lady Maria to Hyde Park. Lady Maria went up to her room for a pelisse and bonnet, and returned with Gwen in tow. Lord Daventon guessed it was because he had a closed carriage. Drat it, he would have to get a curricle soon, and use Barrington's until then.

He walked with Lady Maria on his arm along the Serpentine, with Gwen trailing after them. While she made amiable conversation, all he could think about was the Interrupted Kiss.

"Shall we return, my lord? You appear rather preoccupied," Lady Maria said.

"I was thinking about my library. I have a new book I want to show you."

"Now? That will be most agreeable."

Lady Maria told Gwen his lordship was taking her to see Lady Daventon, and if she had chores, she needn't come. They would leave her at Severn House, and drive on to Daventon House. Gwen assured her she had all the time and would like above all to accompany her. It would give her an opportunity to meet the staff, they were all newly recruited, and seeing that Lady Maria was engaged to his lordship, she wanted to make their acquaintance.

Lord Daventon, his good humor remarkably restored, kept Lady Maria and Gwen entertained with sundry topics of their interest. At Daventon House, he summoned a footman to take Gwen to the housekeeper.

"We can safely tell Laura's debut is a success. She has many callers," Lady Maria said, pausing at the door to the morning room.

"We must leave her to them. My mother and aunt will be with her."

Lady Maria disregarded him and went in. After a moment's hesitation, Lord Daventon followed. Lady Laura was surrounded by young tulips, one of them reciting his Ode to Lovely Laura. A fair number of society matrons were come to renew their acquaintance with Lady Daventon and Lady Helena.

Lord Daventon's hope of spending a private moment with his betrothed did not come to pass. Lady Maria stayed beside Lady Daventon until the last caller left.

But he was not easily swayed from his purpose. "Mother, I have something to discuss with Lady Maria," he said, and led her purposefully into the library.

Lady Maria was not amused. "Why did you lock the door? What will your mother think? And the servants? They'll gossip, for sure."

Lord Daventon didn't deign to give an answer. He took Lady Maria's flushed face in his hands and looked into her eyes. Satisfied that her indignant words belied her inclination, he kissed her, to find the soft, pliable mouth mutinously shut.

"Please," he coaxed, and Lady Maria relented, the laughter in her eyes giving way to desire.

She sighed and Lord Daventon deepened the kiss, the fingers of one hand buried in Lady Maria's luxuriant hair, while cradling her closer with the other hand.

He came to himself when Lady Maria started pushing him away. "Gareth! Someone's knocking! My hairpins! I can't face anyone like this!"

In a daze, Lord Daventon went down on all fours, searching for errant hairpins. Lady Maria thrust them into the hurried chignon she had managed to create.

Gareth opened the door. Lady Daventon and Lady Helena looked at him disapprovingly and marched in. They wanted dear Maria to dine with them, they said, and help them choose what to wear for the evening literary soiree they were all attending.

It took a few days before Lord Daventon learned to run his courtship along approved lines. He found he could spend an entire afternoon in Lady Maria's exclusive company as long as he left the door open by a few inches. He could draw her apart at a picnic without raising eyebrows provided they remained in sight of the other guests. His smart new curricle arrived within a week, and he took his lady love riding at the fashionable hour. He claimed the waltz and the supper dance at all the society events they attended.

Lord Daventon discovered that if one had an amount of ingenuity and the lady was willing, one could steal a fair number of kisses even under the watchful gaze of the *ton*. He was no slow top and Lady Maria was demurely willing. She developed a penchant for carrying a handful of hairpins in her reticule, and for leaving off wearing her gloves when she traveled with Lord Daventon in a closed carriage.

Lord Daventon learned to play lady's maid.

Their understanding of geometry helped them in calculating the minimum linear and angular distance between two bodies so as not to noticeably crush a gentleman's neckcloth.

While they did manage to slip away now and then, they spent a considerable time talking. For the first time in his life, Daventon revealed how betrayed and forsaken he had felt when as a boy, his mother had disappeared from his life.

"Sometimes I blamed my mother for leaving us, at other times I was furious my father had let her go. In a way I lost both parents. Aunt Nell did her best, bless her, but I never spoke to her about my mother. It felt disloyal."

Lady Maria told him about her childhood hurts.

"I grew up fighting my mother's battles. I imagined a slight even when there was none. Though I was but a child, it stung that everyone disparaged my mother. I wanted to prove that the daughter of a commoner could better them all. I wanted to gain the *ton*'s approval and toss it aside, and sail to America. It seems foolish and rather vengeful, doesn't it?"

"It doesn't. Had you received love and warmth, you wouldn't have pined for your childhood home."

"Now I have you, and your love. It matters not where my home is," Lady Maria said, blinking back sudden tears.

She still wanted the plantation but her happiness did not depend on it. A lot had changed. Lady Severn had given her the letters her father had written as a boy and a young man. While she did not possess anything belonging to her mother, she had received a letter from her mother's brother. He was in America and would be attending her wedding. Laura had truly become her sister. Lady Daventon and Lady Helena showered her with affection.

Daventon raised her hand to his lips and waited for her to compose herself. "Meyers has assigned the task to an attorney in America. We will do everything possible to buy the plantation back."

"I know," Lady Maria said.

"If we can't buy it back, we'll visit and pay our respects."

"I know," Lady Maria said, lacing her fingers with Gareth's and resting her head against his shoulder.

"I love you, you know."

Lady Maria looked up with a mischievous smile. "I know. I also know I shall be marrying a laggard."

It took a moment before his lordship understood her meaning. The other guests had wandered away from the picnic spot to follow their own inclinations and they were alone.

"I'm no laggard, my lady," he said and set upon the gratifying task of proving it.

# Epilogue

Before the Season ended, the Daventon family returned to their manor in the country. Their happiness that Lady Daventon was back in her rightful home was tempered with the sorrow that the late earl was no longer with them. At Lady Helena's suggestion, invitations for the wedding were also sent to those friends and relatives with whom he had severed contact because he had also missed them.

The first guest to arrive was also the most eagerly awaited one. Mr. Thornton was Lady Maria's maternal uncle. After living for several years on the Continent, he had recently moved to America. Until two months ago, he had believed that his niece had perished along with her parents in the contagion.

Lord Russell was another guest who received a very warm welcome. He was a part of Lady Helena's growing years and the brother of her dearest friend. She was delighted to see him. He was even more pleased than her, so much so that five weeks later he was walking down the aisle with her.

The Duchess of Severn and Lady Maria arrived two days before the wedding. They brought some of their close friends.

On the eve of the wedding, after the sumptuous feast, the younger guests contrived to have dancing because it was rare for musicians from London to play in their neighborhood.

Laura was distracted all through the wedding arrangements and festivities. First because she was worried that the Duke of Wimberley would not come, and after his arrival, that he barely noticed her. The man was infuriatingly daft. He treated her as if she was still the little girl he had met years ago. She wanted to dance with him but he was oblivious and stood talking with a group of men.

Vexed beyond measure, she marched up to him and tapped his arm. "Your Grace?" The duke turned away from the men. "Lady Laura," he murmured. She had not given a thought to what she would say except that she was angry that he would not look at her while she had thought of him for weeks. "Will you dance the waltz with me?" she blurted out.

***

The wedding day dawned bright and clear. As the parish church was small, only a few close friends accompanied the family to the wedding ceremony. The Duke of Wimberley was among them. He was also performing the office of groomsman.

Lady Maria's gown was an exquisite creation of pale pink satin and a gauzy silver material. For all its fine embroidery and workmanship, it paled in comparison to the bride's radiant face. She sparkled as she walked up the aisle on her uncle's arm.

The ceremony was long and at times the bride and groom appeared not to be giving it their full attention. Not so when they made their vows. Lord Daventon spoke them in a loud and determined voice, his eyes fixed on his bride's face with a look that promised to love and cherish her forever. Maria's voice was softer, as if she was in a trance or living a dream.

Lady Daventon and Lady Helena were seen to frequently apply their handkerchiefs to their optics. Gwen was openly shedding tears.

And the Duchess of Severn was heard to sniff in a most unladylike manner.

## About Jessica Spencer

Jessica Spencer a.k.a Gita V. Reddy is a multi genre author who writes fiction for all ages. Friday's Child by Georgette Heyer lured her into reading regency romances. After devouring all of Ms Heyer's books she went on to read books other regency authors but Georgette Heyer, with her unique blend of fun, humor, romance, and intrigue, remained a firm favorite. Sisters by Marriage is her debut series. For more details about the author, please visit her website https://www.gitavreddy.com

## Other Books in the Series

### Not Just Lovely Laura

Growing up in the shadow of her parents' estrangement, Laura has learnt to mask her feelings. She is also unused to company. Her father, though an earl, was a recluse.

Now she must go to London during the Season where she will meet her mother - the mother she had pined for and resented in equal measure.

Laura finds herself a success. She has suitors offering for her but is secretly in love with the Duke of Wimberley. She isn't sure about his feelings. Does it even matter? The duke is most attentive to the beautiful widow, Lady Mannering.

And then Laura learns a shocking truth about the duke. He is not the man he appears to be.

Anthony, Duke of Wimberley is in London to find a wife for the second time. Seven years ago he had made a love match. He knows better now. He is looking for someone who will take charge of the duties of duchess and also be a mother to his daughter.

His intention to guard his heart disappears as he comes to know Laura. Before he can proceed to court her, he becomes mired in perhaps the biggest Scandal of all time.

To his utter shock, not only does Lady Laura believe the worst about him, she goes out of her way to thwart him!

## No Longer Flighty Fanny

As a young girl, Fanny finds escape from her unstable home by roaming in the woods and riding her mare. Free and innocent of guile, she is easy prey for a blackguard. Three years later, she attends the Season where she meets Andrew, Earl of Nethercote. It is love at first sight for both of them.

Fanny's nemesis, the man who had ruined her, is also in London. Furious at her refusal to yield to him, he uses his power to vilify her. Fanny loses her reputation - and Andrew's love. She returns home and her father forces her into a repugnant marriage.

Andrew leaves England and throws himself into the shipping business. Unable to forget Fanny, he comes back when she is widowed and tries his utmost to win her back.

Can Fanny forgive him for leaving her? And what of the anonymous letters that threaten to destroy her if she accepts Andrew?

## Never Silly Sophie

Used to a lifetime of neglect, Sophie is still shocked when her mother disowns her. Where is she to go in London, a city that is wholly new to her?

Fortunately, a chain of events dramatically changes her life. Sophie finds new friends and is reunited with her brother, the Earl of Nethercote. She also falls in love. But at heart she is still Silly Sophie. How can she compete against the alluring lady who has gentlemen falling over her?

Christopher, the Duke of Henderson has had enough of being pursued by women. When his lackey informs him that a young woman was found in his carriage house and claims to have lost her memory, he is incensed.

But when the frightened young woman in a dirt-stained gown is presented to him, he knows she is no conniving female. Babbling of kings and dukes, she is most likely missing a few marbles!

At first intrigued and then entranced by Sophie's honest feelings, Christopher must guard his love from dangers unforeseen and from the scheming and vicious Lady Dorothea who is determined to become his duchess.

# Rescuing Miss Fairfax
## Book 1 – Season of Love
An eligible earl and a vicar's daughter fall in love,
but there are those who scheme to drive them apart…

Abigail Fairfax is a spirited young lady who often acts on impulse, much to her own regret. When she encounters Richard, the handsome Earl of Ransbury, in an unconventional situation, she is both mortified and intrigued. Richard, on the other hand, is captivated by her frankness and wit. He finds himself drawn to her. Abby is also attracted to Richard. She feels at ease in his company, and loves that he makes her forget that he is an earl.

Soon, Richard and Abby are deeply in love. But before they can get engaged, Abby falls prey to a malicious scheme to tarnish her reputation. Richard believes her unfaithful, and Abby is left heartbroken and alone.

Months later, they meet again during the London Season. They pretend to be indifferent, but their feelings are still strong. Richard tries to find a suitable bride among the other debutantes, while Abby encourages a match between Richard and her friend.

Meanwhile, another plot to destroy Abby is brewing …

Made in the USA
Columbia, SC
30 January 2024